THE MINDER

BENJAMIN J SAWYER

STONE & IVY PUBLISHING

Stone & Ivy Publishing

www.benjaminjsawyer.com

For Dion, always.

PROLOGUE

HER NAME WAS JESSICA. Nineteen years old and studying to be a midwife. Facts that were sure to be repeated by the newspapers and plastered all over social media when her body was found. Facts that meant nothing to the man now standing over her.

That is not to say that his intentions there were at all driven by sexual desire. The truth, in fact, was quite different. It was not that he did not find her attractive; it had been her physical characteristics that had drawn his gaze to begin with. Her hair, which had once flowed so freely down her back, and was now covering a sizeable portion of the slate tiled floor, was a fiery scarlet red. You could have easily mistaken it for the nest of a great bird of prey, and it was in stark contrast to the complexion of her skin. An almost doll-like white that accented deep, dark eyes and laid the foundation for the scattering of subtle freckles that covered the entirety of her trim, athletic physique.

· · ·

THE SCENT OF HER PERFUME, however, and how the September moonlight from the window kissed her hair, brought his skin to gooseflesh. It was not an expensive floral, like the girl before her had worn, but a subtle, almost musky scent, with just a playful hint of vanilla. That, together with their combined presence there, in that dank, stone walled cottage, had his breathing ever so slightly elevated, and the contents of his trousers growing.

1

_____

Detective Inspector Graham Walker tapped the index finger of his right hand on the top of his steering wheel in a musical, but clearly anxious, rhythm. The vehicles in front of his own had been at a standstill now for nearly ten minutes.

He sat in commuter limbo, in what was the only constant he now had left in his life besides work. A 1998 Jeep Cherokee that, like its owner, was showing signs of wear and tear.

As a twenty-three-year veteran of South Wales Police, he had been involved in the investigation of an array of heinous crimes over the years, from working the beat as a junior uniformed officer to more recent atrocities that had come across his desk as a detective. The recent disappearances, however, troubled him greatly. For reasons that he could not yet fully comprehend, these cases gave him the chills –

something that he had rarely experienced in his forty-eight years.

Graham wound down his driver's side window and invited into the car the orchestra that was central Cardiff at peak rush hour: a symphony of sirens, construction sites and manic, impatient motorists. It was almost deafening. And for most, would have been bordering on unbearable. But not for him. For Graham, the unrelenting noise of the city was a comfort, a constant distraction that helped to drown out the problems that plagued his daily thoughts. And that was most welcome.

Patting the pockets of his well-worn, mock-tweed suit jacket, he found and then withdrew a half-empty packet of cigarettes. He pulled one out with his lips, lighting it with the car's lighter in a single, swift movement.

"Any bloody time now would be great," he said, his husky voice failing to hide his building agitation.

Exhaling a cloud of blue smoke towards the windscreen, he closed his eyes and rubbed his forehead with the ends of his weathered fingers. The lit end of the cigarette coming dangerously close to singeing his greying hair.

Not an unattractive man in his youth, he was looking now somewhat haggard. His eyes, which had been a striking feature of his earlier years, a piercing blue that saw straight through you, were now cradled in permanent dark bags. A symptom, no doubt, of his drinking. That of late, had ushered towards the heavier side of social. Something that had not gone unnoticed by friends, colleagues, or his recently estranged wife.

That, and being kept awake by next door's constant cycle of arguments and make up sex, he thought. Olivia had got the house in the divorce, and he was currently living in a rundown mid-terrace in a less-than-ideal part of the city.

The relative calm of the day's sixth cigarette was abruptly interrupted by the vibration in the left pocket of his trousers. Holding the remaining half of the cigarette in his lips, he reached for his phone.

Incoming call – Reed.

Graham rolled his eyes as he blew smoke from his nose like an urban, twentieth century dragon. He slid his finger across the screen, answered, tapping the loudspeaker icon as he placed the phone face-up on his thigh.

"Grayo, where the sodding hell have you been?" demanded a soft voice.

That voice, the voice radiating from Graham's left leg, belonged to his partner of the last two years, Lewis Reed – Detective Sergeant Lewis Reed.

Lewis was the archetypal poster boy copper. There were no other words for it. He had joined the police fresh from university, where he'd studied history and politics, and had served faultlessly in uniform. As he had continued to do since transferring to CID. Lewis had personally requested to work alongside Graham, and had been at his side ever since.

"I've been trying to reach you all morning..." he continued.

That was true. If his math was correct, Graham surmised that this was the fourth time Lewis had called that day. The first had woken him. The second and third calls he had merely ignored, while trying to compose himself and put on trousers.

As of that morning, it had been roughly eight weeks since Graham's marriage to Olivia had been legally over. A messy divorce, plagued with accusations of infidelity on her part and drunken disregard on his. He had not taken it well. Not only was he no longer a resident in the family four bed, which he claimed he paid for, but his best friend of five years, Willow, an English Cocker Spaniel, had to stay as well. And that, quite rightly, hurt him more than anything. The entire experience had left a lingering, unpleasant taste in his mouth. Not that he was bitter or anything.

As a result, and to help drown out his neighbours' nightly acrobatics, Graham had taken solace in alcohol. Beer, if he had remembered to go to the shops. Otherwise, anything wet and strong sufficed. Nursing a permanent, lingering hangover, his professional life, as well as social, was suffering. Getting out of bed now was a mammoth task by itself.

The timing could not have been worse. A little over a year ago, ramblers had discovered the body of a young woman. She had been stripped naked and hastily dumped on the side of a country lane. The postmortem pronounced death by asphyxiation. Someone had strangled her. The way in which she was discovered suggested that it was not just a crime of passion or a random act. Upon examination, no DNA or any other evidence was found on or around her body, bar a few partial fingerprints on her throat and wrists. The only silver lining, if it could be considered so, was that there was no reason to indicate she had been sexually assaulted before or after death. Due to the lack of suspects, a clear motive, or at the very least, evidence, the case had gone as cold as her corpse.

That was until the reported disappearance of a nineteen-year-old university student the past weekend. Graham could not help but notice the similarities in the girls' appearance. Their reported last movements were fearfully alike as well. Afraid that a single perpetrator, or even a copycat, could be responsible, he had submitted his findings to his immediate superior, expecting to be laughed out of the office. Although initially sceptical, DCI Stephen

Morgan, a man who Graham's female colleagues described as a *misogynistic prick*, charged him to investigate further. The last thing Morgan had said they needed was a copycat ripper on the loose, and Graham could not have agreed more.

It was reading of crimes, such as those of Peter Sutcliffe and, closer to home, of John William Cooper, that had inspired Graham to join the police as a young boy. He hoped, deep in his bones, that this phone call was not what he feared.

"I'll be there in a bit, Lewis." He groaned, now rubbing the side of his face, carpeted with day-ten stubble. "My alarm didn't go off; you know what I'm like with this bloody phone."

"Be where, the station? Fuck sake mate, don't you read your emails either?" Lewis replied, half joking.

Graham had not opened his phone this morning, let alone read any emails. The fact that he was wearing matching socks he considered a miracle.

"You might want to turn yourself around," Lewis said, sounding a little patronising. "Meet me in the car park for the Pen Pych mountain trail."

Graham swallowed hard, dreading the next words to come out of Lewis Reed's mouth. He searched with his right hand for his remaining cigarettes, unaware that the packet had fallen into the footwell of his car. He knew the trail well – a picturesque corner of Wales. A place where he and Olivia had often hiked during the infancy of their relationship. A place where their love had blossomed between the spring flowers and the winding streams. They had planned their life together here, and Graham had even proposed. And he wondered what the hell Lewis was doing there.

"Do you need me to send you directions?" Lewis asked.

"Nope," he replied with all the enthusiasm he could muster. "I know where you are. I'll be with you shortly."

Graham searched the traffic ahead for a way out of the standstill. Up ahead, a left turn, barely one hundred yards away. There was a drive through café on this road, he knew, and a quick coffee stop would be most welcome.

"Oh, and Graham, bring your game face," Lewis continued. "It's the Evans girl... we think we've found her."

2

THESE PEOPLE I SEE HERE, surrounding me as they do, Monday through Friday, are idiots. Each and every one of them is a testament to the fact that there should be a lifeguard in the gene pool, Jackson thought to himself, as he sat at his desk, smiling politely at his colleagues as they went about their day.

Jackson Page was liked by the people he worked alongside. They revered him for his skill and imagination, although many of his peers considered him something of an anomaly. He was notably absent from social media. The only mention of him anywhere online was in fact the *meet the team* page on the company website. And that was not by choice. He avoided the frequent company nights out. He avoided drinking entirely, but made an effort to show up at the annual Christmas party, or at a funeral. He was someone who kept his business to himself; and that was the way he liked it.

Jackson did not dislike people as a rule. He found it hard to separate what he considered negative personality traits, or aspects of someone's lifestyle, from the person themselves. As a result, he worked hard to give people a shining impression of himself. He was well spoken, polite, well dressed and concerned with *your* problems. He was everyone's friend. He was *your* friend.

A shining example of his feeling towards his colleagues, and the local population in general, was the thirty-something year-old peacocking his way towards Jackson's workstation. Joel Saunders. Jackson's line manager and the nephew of one of the company's directors. A guy who possessed the type of non-descript northern accent that only the producers of a reality television show could love. With the bravado and overly tight T-shirt to match.

"Jackie, bro. We still cool for that lift later on tonight?"

Honestly, Joel, we're using "bro" now? Jackson thought, rolling his eyes internally.

The event in question was a book launch. A fantasy novel, written by an aspiring local author. Jackson normally illustrated children's books, but after reading the synopsis for the novel, he relished the opportunity to submit a design for the cover. Both the writer and publisher loved his composition. As a result, an invitation to attend the launch had been emailed to the office. He jumped at the chance to meet the author and to be surrounded by people who he hoped could offer conversation that extended beyond last night's television programming, or who Gemma from accounting was sleeping with behind her girlfriend's back. Joel's reasons for going, however, to Jackson at least, were less clear. He was confident that Joel had never even held a book. Let alone read one.

"It's going be crawling with nerdy birds, mate. Dark rimmed glasses, that intelligent look, the full scene," Joel said with a laddish snigger.

Charming, Jackson thought, trying with all of his might not to punch Joel square in the jugular. He was within range, after all.

"Sure," he replied, trying to emulate some of Joel's confidence. "I'm sure it will be a laugh."

For me, at least.

Jackson had been at his current job now for a few years. It was the second firm he had worked for since university, the first since his failed attempt at going freelance. There, at least the projects were almost guaranteed. The firm had an excellent reputation and, for now at least, Jackson himself was in demand. There were more pressing matters to worry about than putting food in the fridge. For now, this position was ideal.

He continued to exchange pleasantries with Joel for a few moments before he was called away. For what, Jackson did not know, or particularly care. He was not entirely sure what Joel's role there was. That was, besides procrastination, and thinly veiled sexual advances towards their female peers. Perks, Jackson assumed, of being the company director's spoilt nephew. Jackson himself resisted urges to explore anything more than platonic relationships as often as he could. His last two had expired early on. They had failed to outlive the excitement that accompanies a fledgling relationship, it seems.

There had been news of a girl reported missing that past weekend, and it had been spreading through the office since Monday morning. Worry crossed the face of every woman in the room. Feigned concern on the men's, who, despite appearances, were desperately trying to sleep with them. Jackson had naturally offered sympathetic comments whenever the conversation came his way.

A glowing impression, he thought. *I am your friend, and I care.*

Glad for the brief respite gifted by his colleague's departure, Jackson reached into the backpack, sat to his left, underneath his desk, and seized his headphones from inside. He thumbed the screen of his phone, searching for the perfect playlist. Music helped him work. Helped him focus. Helped him plan.

The ground floor office where his company worked from was encased on all sides, by full height windows with spectacular views. He was glad for the natural light. Much roomier and less dreary than some of the places he had worked in the past. *Easier to stay motivated over long periods of time*, he thought, *when you do not feel like a caged animal.*

Satisfied with his selection, Jackson turned to the computer on his desk and began to work. He was adding the finishing touches to an outstanding project. An illustration for the cover of a children's book due for release at the end of the year. The book was about a courageous calf and his misadventures with a pair of foolish but loveable piglets. Cute, and sure to be a hit with boys and girls the country over.

"This one is for you." he said in a whispering breath, smiling to himself as he pressed the save icon on the screen. "I do hope you like it."

As the day's fading sun peered over the top of his monitor, it dazzled him slightly, and he shielded his eyes. Jackson laughed to himself at the prospect of Joel at the book launch, meandering aimlessly in the crowd, as out of place as a hippo at a racetrack, and just as majestic. He just hoped, deep to his bones, that Joel would not make a fool of them both that evening.

3

———

THE DAY WAS COLD. Not the temperature per se, although there was a chill in the air, but the contrast. Like looking through a grey, filtered lens. Gravel crunched underfoot as Graham made his way across the car park. The normally tranquil spot, reserved for walkers and birdwatchers, now buzzed with activity. Lewis was waiting at the far end, coffee in hand, a tooth mark-embellished pen balancing from his lips.

The surrounding hills, fringed in towering pines, sheltered the car park from the worst of the weather. Clouds were gathering overhead. A pristine backdrop for the bleak day ahead.

"She was found in the early hours," Lewis said flatly. "By a group of teenagers who were up here, drinking, or god only knows what."

His eyes searched Graham's face for a sense of where he was within himself that morning. He was a difficult man to read at the best of times, and today was no different. The addition of sunglasses made Lewis' task even harder still.

"I hope you're well rested this morning," Lewis resumed with a hint of sarcasm in his voice. "She's over here."

He motioned to an area of long grass behind them. A group of Scenes of Crime Officers were busy setting up photography equipment. And another, standing off to the side, was talking dryly into a Dictaphone.

Not thirty yards from the edge of the car park, as if situated, in waiting for public display, like a piece from a depraved art exhibition, were the near unspoilt remains of Miss Jessica Evans. Positioned, lying on her back, her one open eye looking skyward towards the heavens. Her scarlet hair was sodden from the morning rain.

Near unspoilt. The dainty form that would have once been her throat had been carved open from one side to the other to look like a ghostly jester's smile. It would not have taken an expert to have deduced that she would have bled out like livestock. And the lack of any blood at the scene made Graham's veins run cold.

That alone would have been enough, but the fact that half of her face was covered by what seemed to be a cow mask, had raised a collective eyebrow or two among those who were present. As murder scenes went, this one was special.

"Morning, Graham," one of the techs said, and the others nodded almost in unison, as if to echo the greeting, and went about their duties.

"Jesus, what the hell is this?" Graham said quietly, with an expressionless face. The question required no answer, he knew the twisted pile lying at his feet matched the missing girl's description perfectly.

She had been laid out like a renaissance maiden posing

for a painting. She was stark naked, except for the mask, and Graham thought that as twisted as the killer must have been, they at least had some class. It almost appeared that they had tried to protect the girl's modesty. Her left hand was down, covering her genitals. Her right arm across her chest, covering her breasts. The only outward sign of trauma, her neck aside, was the bruising around her wrists and ankles. That looked as though it had been branded there.

"Bastard didn't want her to breathe again, it seems," one of the forensic officers remarked, almost smirking. She reached out a hand to Graham in greeting.

"Always under the best of circumstances, Ainsley," he jested dryly, shaking her hand. "How have you been?"

Ainsley was the force's lead pathologist. She and Graham had worked countless cases together over the years, running from the mundane to the damn right obscene. And some that were just plain horrific.

"Better than you, I would say, Gray. You look like shit," she replied, returning the dry quip. Lewis smirked to himself. Graham caught it from the corner of his eye and shot the young sergeant a sideways glance, raising an eyebrow.

"Have you ever come across anything like this?" Graham asked, posing the question to Ainsley alone.

"No. Not in work at least," she said. "I haven't seen meat this clean and dry since the last time I went to the butchers for a pack of steaks and a stuffed chicken."

Lewis gagged and turned away from the group in an attempt to save face as Ainsley's colleagues took photographs of the scene. It was as if they were admiring Jessica's form from every angle. She looked like a model, taking part in a posthumous shoot for some ghostly portfolio.

"The area's clean," she continued. "As is she, the girl was moved here after the fact. Not that I needed to point that out. And whoever did it did a bloody good job at making our lives harder. There is bugger all to work with. Not even a sodding footprint."

Silence fell upon them as Graham glared down at the body. He rubbed the stubble on his face to the sound of sandpaper on timber. His eyes darted left, and then right, taking in every detail of the scene before him. And it made him feel sick. Bile made its way northwards towards his throat as his mind cast back and recalled images from a crime scene from a year before. Another young girl. Another non-descript lane in the countryside.

Jesus, not again, he thought.

"Why the mask?" Lewis asked, his voice cutting through the quiet.

Graham scoffed. "Why do any of it?"

Lewis turned to him with a look of bemusement, holding his mouth slightly agape.

"What I mean to say..." Graham continued, with his eyes still fixed on the girl "...is why bother with all the faff afterwards? It's because it's a part of their fun. A part of their process. Why the mask? Beats me, but my guess is that it means something to them. And that's where we come in. To find out."

He took a crumpled packet of cigarettes from his pocket and lit one, allowing the cloud of blue smoke to drift away effortlessly on the morning breeze. He drew in a lungful of the crisp air and let it all out in a slow, purposeful sigh.

"Any witnesses that we know of, apart from the group that found her?" he asked.

"None. Just them." Lewis pointed to a group of youths standing next to a patrol car, speaking to a uniformed officer.

"Shall we have a little chat?"

"Gray," Ainsley called out, as he and Lewis turned and made for the group. "What about her parents?"

"They will have to be notified, and will need to formally identify her when you're finished. We'll swing by later and you can brief us in full then as well. Give me a call when you're ready."

She nodded in agreement, smiled at him with an adoring gaze, as she always did, and went about her duties. Graham had never been able to return the affection, as much as he had wanted to. He thought a lot of Ainsley. She was intelligent, beautiful, and had an astonishing sense of humour. As rocky as his marriage had been in recent years, however, he would never have strayed. A courtesy not extended back his way, unfortunately.

Maybe I'll ask her out, he thought to himself, smiling as he and Lewis made their way to the group of teenage witnesses. Lewis could not help but notice the uncharacteristic delight on his face, but in better judgement, decided not to mention anything.

The group of youths, two boys and a girl, roughly sixteen years of age, were clearly sobering up from the worst hangover of their lives. It was unclear what was worse, stumbling across a murder victim or the dull headache from a shared, five-pound bottle of vodka.

"Apart from the obvious," Graham began, "did you lot see anything out of the ordinary?"

The group exchanged uncomfortable looks. The larger of the two lads, wearing a matching grey tracksuit, looked as though he was about to break down in tears.

"There was a car," the girl said from underneath a base-ball cap, as she wiped snot from her nose. "It was just sat in this car park with its engine on, in the dark."

Graham's ears pricked up, and he shot a glance at Lewis.

"When we got closer, to the bird on the floor I mean, its lights came on and it drove off," the shorter of the two boys said.

Lewis ushered Graham away, out of earshot of the group.

"The ramblers who found Sophie last year mentioned a car doing something similar," he said. "It wasn't in their statements, but I remember one of the lads mentioning it at the time."

"What did this car look like?" Graham turned and posed the question to the group, pointing at them with the lit end of his cigarette.

"Dunno, mate, it was dark. It was long, like an estate car, and dark. Like red or grey or something," the lad in the grey said, visibly anxious. "Look, mate, are we in trouble? My mum will kill me if she finds out I've been caught drinking again."

Seeming to brush off the boy's last statement, Graham turned to his partner, his face full of electricity. Any sign of the morning's earlier grogginess had dissipated, and in its place stood a man with drive and a purpose.

"Lewis, did you bring your car?"'

"No, why? I jumped in with..."

"GREAT, come with me then. We need to see the DCI. He's going to want to hear about this."

4
_____

THE BOY with the blue backpack walked alone across the playground. The blood under his left nostril was fresh, just like the bruise on his cheek. He had lost the fight, which ended ten minutes ago, and he was sure to lose the one waiting for him when he got home. It started to rain a little; he looked up as droplets of water pitter-pattered on his forehead. One tracked the length of his face, mixing with the blood, and entered his mouth. It tasted like a spoon, he thought. And as the rain continued to fall, he walked faster.

HE HAD no friends on the playground. His friends were on the stacks and shelves, between the pages, pictures, and words of the books in the library, where he was heading now. They did not judge him, call him names, or beat him. They did not laugh at him when he was on the floor, face down in a puddle, crying. They instead, comforted him, and transported him to wondrous places, far away from the misery of every day. Places he felt safe. Places he felt loved. For him, the dusty grey carpet, in the far-left corner of the library, next to the free-standing globe and geography books, felt like home.

5

THE OFFICE DOOR was already open when Graham and Lewis reached the far end of the corridor. Graham had phoned ahead from the car, and upon reaching the door, could see that Detective Chief Inspector Stephen Morgan was ready and waiting for them, sitting behind the desk in the centre of the sparsely decorated room. A tall, potted monstera was positioned to his right, on top of an aged, blue carpet that had seen more than its fair share of years underfoot. The only comfort adorning the office, apart from the bottle of whisky that Morgan kept tucked away in a drawer next to his left leg, were photos of his family, which were positioned across the front of his desk, dressed in cheap wooden frames.

DCI Morgan was a short, thickset man in his late fifties. He wore an oddly shaped moustache and was certainly balding. Something that he did not hide well. He seemed to be visibly unwell. Always struggling for breath when he moved more than a few yards and uncomfortably red in the face when getting worked up or stressed. Due to a lifetime of abusing fast food, beer, and women, Graham thought. Contrary to what the DCI himself told people.

Morgan raised the palm of his hand to the pair as they entered, as if to cut them off before they had even spoken. He looked down towards his desk and cradled his large fore-head in his other hand. Letting out a long sigh, he looked up at the pair. And through eyes that screamed exhaustion, he attempted to smile.

"What a mess, hey lads," he said. "The press is going to bloody love this one. I can already see it now. They are going to label this sick bastard something like 'the masking madman' or something else completely unimaginative to really get the public all riled up."

Morgan sat back in his chair and cast his gaze to the ceil-ing. His expression told the other two men that he wished to be anywhere else. Anywhere, but in a drab corner office, discussing the finer points of murder with his colleagues before lunch.

He continued, "You mentioned a car, Graham. What was that about?"

"The group who found her. Who found Miss Evans..." he added, consulting his notepad, "...described seeing a dark car loitering around near the scene."

Morgan grunted in response, and gestured for him to continue.

"Not only that, sir, but Detective Reed kindly reminded me that the poor couple who came across Sophie Jones last year..."

Morgan snapped to attention, his eyes widening. "Sophie?"

"Yes, sir. They mentioned something similar. But the details of that we would need to clarify."

Graham leaned into Morgan. So close, in fact, that he could smell the whisky on his old partner's breath. Close enough that he could drop his voice to a whisper.

"The girls, sir. Are very similar in both appearance and age..."

"Jesus, Gray," Morgan said, startling even himself with the volume of his voice. "We all know how it looks."

"Sir, if I may..."

Morgan raised his hand, cutting Graham off, tapping his other fingers to a file on his desk.

"But, before *this* goes any further, we need to get our facts straight." He paused for a second, half expecting one of the detectives before him to interject. "We have unsolved cases coming out of our arses, and this is the last thing we need."

The small room fell silent. Graham and Lewis exchanged looks of concern but said nothing. They both knew the financial constraints of the department. And that in terms of manpower, they were stretched to their limits. But still. The images of earlier that day, images of that broken and twisted young girl, came flooding into Graham's mind. And the mask. How could he ever forget that mask?

Morgan's voice once again boomed as he stood from behind his desk. It seemed to echo from every surface in the room, as if it reverberated through Graham's body, deep to his bones.

"I cannot go upstairs, or worse yet, go public, with fantasies of a would-be serial killer without some concrete proof. I, no, we..." Morgan motioned to the pair "...would be a bloody laughing-stock."

Morgan took a few deep breaths, sitting back down and closing his eyes. He leaned back in his chair and folded his hands in his lap. His breathing slowed. And with each consecutive laboured breath, his pent-up anger dispersed. He opened his eyes and looked at Graham, his face now conveying worry and guilt simultaneously. His voice became softer now, too.

"Have you been to see Ainsley yet?" he asked.

"No sir, I'm still waiting on her call," Graham replied.

"Okay. Well, that seems like as good as any place to start. Then pop round and have a word with the old codgers from Sophie's case tomorrow, see if their description of the car matches ours from today."

Morgan stood up from behind his desk, turned his back on the two detectives, and stared out of the window and into the car park below. The glass dripped with beads of condensation, fogging up more and more each time Morgan took a breath.

"If it is them, the same killer, then we have failed Jessica and her family. We cannot let that happen again," Morgan said. "I hope to god you're wrong, Grayo. I really do."

He turned back to them and pointed a chubby finger at the pair.

"Can you handle it, lads? I've got a briefing in twenty minutes and the victims from the Blackmore case won't become magically un-raped. Least we can do is catch that sick fucker and give *them* some closure."

Graham and Lewis nodded in unison.

"On it, sir," Graham replied, standing and turning for the door.

"Oh, and Graham."

"Sir?"

"Keep me in the loop this time."

THE ONLY WARMTH in the room was the smile she gifted to him. Her face lit up as he crossed the threshold of the clinical, unwelcoming space. The smell hit him before the cold. There was no masking the scent of death. It came at him, embraced him, and the stench brought tears to his eyes.

The glow on her face was unusual, considering the task she had just undertaken. Ainsley stood by her desk, scribbling notes onto a clipboard. Jessica's body lay not six feet away, covered to the neck in a crisp, white sheet. She looked at peace, calmer somehow, than when he had last seen her.

"There's not a whole lot I can tell you that you don't already know," Ainsley said bluntly. "Cardiac arrest was brought on by massive blood loss. The wound on her neck says it all really, I'm afraid."

"Any sign of other injuries?" Graham asked, approaching her desk.

"Nothing major, apart from the bruising and some minor torn flesh on her wrists and ankles. Nothing to indicate she was raped though, thank god." She walked over to Jessica, pulled back the sheet and held up a porcelain hand. "It doesn't seem as though she put up a fight, either. Nothing under her fingernails to suggest much of a struggle. But then, she is unusually clean."

Graham scoffed. "Bleach, like the other one?"

"A lot of it. Not only that, but her hair has been recently washed as well."

Jesus fuck, Graham thought, rubbing the bridge of his nose with his fingers.

"Could that bruising have been caused by restraints of some kind?" he asked.

"Definitely. And given everything else, I wouldn't be surprised if she had been hung upside down and bled like a pig."

He and Lewis had passed Jessica's parents on the way in. The mother was inconsolable, sobbing as they walked down the hallway. The father had his arm around her, trying to offer some comfort as he fought back floods of his own. They had been here to formally identify their daughter. Graham could not imagine the horror they had faced, seeing the doll-like form that had once been their little girl.

"What are the chances that she was already unconscious before that wound was inflicted?" Lewis said.

Returning to her desk, Ainsley picked up the clipboard and flicked through a few pages with a raised eyebrow.

"Nothing shows up on our tox screening, so it's unlikely that she was drugged. Although I personally wouldn't rule it out, new compounds are always being developed."

Lewis winced at the thought. Rohypnol had been the scumbag's drug of choice for many years but was getting harder to find. It was easily detected in blood samples, and many dealers were happy to give up their clients for more lenient punishment, something most coppers knew well.

Graham paced the room like a caged animal. He wanted nothing more than a cigarette and a warm latte. Something eloquent on the television to take his mind away from the present. He turned to Ainsley, however, and asked the question that was gnawing at the back of his mind.

"What are the chances that this is the same killer as before?"

Ainsley took a long moment to answer. And in that space, they could hear nothing more than the soft whir of the air conditioning unit and slow tick of time from the clock on the wall. She gazed into his eyes. Her own seeming to convey the very answer he dreaded.

"LET'S just say that I wouldn't rule it out."

6

THE WORLD'S unlikeliest duo made their way down Cardiff's Queen Street, towards the bookshop holding the event. Jackson was smartly dressed, in tight-fitting black jeans and a long-sleeved white shirt. Joel, on the other hand, looked as though he was ready for a boat party in Magaluf. His chequered, above-the-knee shorts and slogan T-shirt starkly contrasted Jackson's crisp outfit. Jackson thought Joel looked ridiculous. Joel, on the other hand, believed he looked fantastic.

Cardiff was busy, despite it not yet being the weekend. Couples dashed between cover for a bite to eat in one of the city's chic eateries. Shoppers braved the weather for one last deal before the stores closed their doors for the day. The evening was pleasantly warm, but the persistent drizzle made Joel's choice in wardrobe even more questionable in Jackson's mind.

A slender woman in thick-framed glasses greeted the

pair at the door. She checked their names against a list that hung from her clipboard, throwing them each a toothy smile before allowing them to enter. The atmosphere inside was electric. The hype for the title's release showed no obvious signs of dwindling. It felt as though the whole city had turned up.

The store was bustling, and everyone was elegantly dressed. Intelligent conversation and champagne flowed as effortlessly between the stacks and shelves as the light that was cast from the crystal chandeliers above. The author, a pretty young woman in her late twenties, was leaning precariously against a display table, clutching a copy of her book as if the pages themselves were somehow anchoring her to reality. The attention was all on her, and she was clearly struggling with that fact. A feeling that Jackson himself was all too familiar with.

"I'm going to grab myself a drink. You want anything?" Joel asked, surveying the room, his eyes being drawn to the longest legs and lowest-cut dresses. "Some fucking talent here, bro."

Jackson rolled his eyes and smirked. Whether it was at Joel's lewd comment or being referred to as "bro" again, he was not even sure himself.

"I'm good Joel, thank you."

"Suit yourself," he scoffed, patting Jackson on the back as he made a beeline for the closest bartender.

SOMETHING CAUGHT Jackson's attention as he made his way across the gathering. In fact, it was *someone.* Someone he spied from the corner of his eye through the crowd. He thought she was glorious. She took his breath away, and she demanded, no, she stole his attention. Her hair was long. It sat just below her breasts and was a striking white blonde; worn in dreadlocks, apart from her fringe, which was cut just above her eyebrows.

Jackson mirrored her movements from across the room, watching her flow effortlessly between the other guests, drink in hand, smiling politely at the conversations around her. The sight of her made his breathing deepen, and he dared not blink for fear of losing sight of her.

She had an intriguing dress sense, Jackson noted. She wore a pair of olive corduroy dungarees, rolled up to accent the heavy, black Dr. Martens boots that adorned her feet. Her wrists were covered in bracelets of all descriptions and colour, and her shoulders were covered by a chequered shirt, rolled to the elbows, exposing the intricate tattooing that wrapped around both her arms and hands. They were locked in a dance that only one partner was currently aware of. And as she was making her way to the buffet table, he altered his course so that he was as well.

A chance meeting.

Over the buzz of the conversation in the store, the sounds of Norah Jones were barely audible in the background. Jackson picked up a plate and filled it. Although unimpressed with the spread, he tried his best to smile politely at the server stationed there; it was not their fault the food was shit after all. He could spare them that much, at least.

He tried to find an opening as she approached the table, a way to initiate a conversation. He opened his mouth, tried to find his words, but she caught him off guard.

"You're the illustrator, aren't you?" she asked. Her voice was soft, welcoming. She reached a hand across the table to greet him with black painted nails. "I'm Elena, Elena Robinson."

"I-I am," he replied with an uncharacteristic stutter that even he, himself, did not see coming. "Jackson..."

"Page, I know," she laughed. "These lot have been talking about your bloody cover all evening. You're a bit of a hit around here."

Her eyes were striking. A vibrant shade of green. Her irises were encircled by a thick black border that emphasised the green it surrounded. He wondered if she might in fact be wearing contact lenses. He could not believe that they were hers, that they were in fact, human.

"Well, I'm not sure about that," he replied sheepishly. "What about you? What's your story?"

"I am the photographer. Well, I'm *a* photographer. I normally focus on lifestyle work. Like skateboarding, surfing, that kind of stuff. But I did the author's portrait for inside the jacket. She's a friend."

"There's not a bad turnout."

His mind was blank at that moment, and he could think of nothing to say. He wanted the ground to swallow him up there and then.

Not a bad turnout, are you fucking stupid?

"Yeah, it's okay," she giggled. "She's had some really good feedback. Considering it's a debut and all. I'm actually surprised. I mean, I'm chuffed for her, but it was unexpected."

He tried to slow his breathing. To give himself a second to gather his thoughts and find his voice.

She's magnificent, is she not? he thought.

Jackson smiled. She wore a ring in the septum of her nose and the light from above glistened from it. He did not want the conversation to die on its face. He had got her this far. He scanned around for something, anything to say, and oddly noticed the lack of meat on her plate.

"Not a fan of the sausage rolls, then?" He felt stupid for even saying it.

You are an idiot.

"Not so much," Elena said, chuckling sweetly. "I prefer animals to people. You see, they don't have the capacity to lie, cheat or steal. They don't manipulate. Their intentions are pure. And for that reason, I would rather keep them in my heart and on my lap, than on my plate."

She picked up a stick of celery from her plate and bit off the end, looking at Jackson with a flirtatious gaze.

"Something we can agree on, then." Jackson matched her celery with a carrot baton and laughed. "People are the worst."

Something inside him stirred. A rush of adrenalin coursed through his veins, and he could feel himself sweating.

Joel re-appeared, as if with impeccably unfortunate timing, a drink in each hand, with a ridiculous smile on his face. In truth, Jackson had almost forgotten he was there, and at that moment he wished more than anything that he were not.

"You've done alright for yourself I see," a clearly half-cut Joel said, again patting Jackson on the back.

This time, however, spilling one of the beverages down the back of his shirt. That pissed Jackson off. But he managed to hide his irritation behind a polite smile and gritted teeth.

"Alright babes, my name's—" Joel said.

"Charmed," Elena said sarcastically, cutting him off and throwing Jackson a grin.

She was captivating, Jackson thought. The way she held herself, the sound of her voice, the shape of her body. He took a depth breath and swallowed hard, struggling again to find his voice. But before he could find any words, she'd jotted her telephone number down on the back of a napkin. She fixed her eyes on his and placed the twice folded serviette into the flat of his hand.

"Well, it's been a pleasure, gentleman," Elena jested. "But I must take my leave."

She walked away and shot a glance over her left shoulder back at Jackson. "Don't wait until Veganuary to help the helpless, Mr Page." With a wide, heartfelt smile and a wink, she melted back into the ocean of bodies.

"Fuck me, she's not bad mate," Joel said, taking a long draw on his drink. Most of it making its way down his chin and T-shirt, and finally onto the floor.

"Yeah, she is something alright." Jackson unfolded the napkin in his hand, revealing her name and phone number, signed off with a single kiss. "Something special indeed."

Isn't she?

7

"Come in, come in officers, out of the cold," the old lady said as she ushered the detectives into her home. She peered out from beyond the door and took a sharp look right, and then left, to see if her neighbours were watching. They were always watching, always judging, she thought.

She followed them down the narrow passageway and directed them right, into her living room, where, seated in a cloth-stitched wingback chair, was an elderly gentleman. The man, who Graham knew to be the lady's husband, was dressed in a neat grey cardigan and beige trousers. His eyes were fixed to the television, a mid-morning game show, so much so that he paid no attention to the two men now standing in his lounge.

"I'll just pop the kettle on, make yourselves at home dears," she said as she moved towards the kitchen. "Would you both like a biscuit?"

"That would be wonderful, thank you," Graham replied.

Her face lit up, and with a shuffle, she was gone.

The house smelt lived in, as though it had been lived in for many years. A welcoming, homely smell that was supported by the scent of baking and the musky scent left by years of memories. It was a smell that complemented the house's décor. Immaculately papered walls sat above soft, patterned carpets. Everywhere Graham looked were lavishly framed and mounted photos of a large extended family, hung on walls and dotted around perfectly polished mahogany furniture. It was by no means modern, no means posh, but it was a home. A proper home. And not at all like the squalor that he himself had been subjected to as of late.

The lady re-appeared moments later carrying a tray laden with tea, biscuits and all manner of scones and cakes. It was all beautifully laid out on what the pair guessed was her best bone china. She was smiling ear to ear; she was a woman who clearly loved to entertain. Graham and Lewis took a seat on the couch as the lady perched herself on the arm of her husband's chair.

"I'm afraid we're here today regarding the murder of Sophie Jones. The girl you found while out walking last year," Graham said.

"Oh, I see," she replied, with a look of shock. "We... well, Brian, gave our statements at the time, didn't you?" Her husband did not seem to be listening, although that did not seem to bother her. She continued. "We gave it to that lovely young man with the ginger hair. I think he was a Scotsman. Tall fellow, think he needed a girlfriend."

The detectives shared a look and Lewis chuckled to himself.

"Yes, we are aware of that, Mrs. Williams." Graham took a sip of tea, then set the cup back on its saucer, leaning closer to the aged woman. "You mentioned a car to one of our colleagues. A car you said seemed to be..." He looked down at his notes before continuing, "...seemed to be hanging around at the time, acting off. But the details never made it into your statement."

"Oh yes, that was rather odd." She clasped her hands under her chin as if in deep thought. "It was like the driver was watching, waiting for us to find the girl, almost. Either that or he was playing with himself. Dirty bastard."

Graham shot Lewis a glance.

"Mrs Williams, could you be so kind and describe the vehicle for us?"

She set her cup down, placed a wrinkled hand on her husband's shoulder, and looked up at Graham and Lewis. The youth of years gone by was still visible behind her hazel eyes. But there was something else too, Graham noticed. Fear? Or guilt, perhaps.

"It was an estate car. A Volvo, I think. And it was a dark. Maybe black." Her voice was trembling slightly.

She looked now solely at Graham, as if she were staring deep into his soul, as if she were asking for his forgiveness.

"The girl," she continued, taking a laboured breath. "We were supposed to have been at the road crossing an hour earlier. It was a planned ramble, you see, but we were so far behind schedule. My knee was playing up a treat that day."

"I'm sorry, Mrs Williams, what has this got to do with the girl?"

"If we were there faster, on time, could we have saved her? Maybe have phoned the police, or an ambulance sooner?"

She was visibly shaking now, and tears were forming in her eyes. She reached for a tissue, but Lewis was there first. He leaned over and handed her one with a pained smile.

"Thank you, dear," she said with a sniffle.

"Mrs. Williams, there would have been nothing you could have done," Graham said sympathetically. "I'm afraid she was gone, many hours before you and your husband arrived."

She searched his face, hoping, praying that what she was hearing was indeed the truth.

Her husband turned now, flipping his gaze from the television set to the detectives. He took his wife's hand in his own and rubbed the top of her weathered fingers tenderly with his thumb.

"You see, officers," he said in a shaky tone. "We lost our Judy in much the same way, some years ago now." His face became sombre as he recalled the memory. "It brought it all back, and Gill and I just wished we could have stopped another family's pain. Thought that maybe we could have helped, that's all."

"Mr. Williams, we are very sorry for the loss of your daughter," Graham replied, "but if you don't mind me asking, how did your daughter die?"

"She was taken from us, Detective Walker. Murdered by her husband and dumped in a field to be a feast for the crows."

Jesus, I wish I hadn't asked.

The elderly couple looked into each other's eyes and nodded. The spark that brought them together all those years ago was so clearly still ablaze in them both. Graham smiled to himself, although inside he was wrought with envy. What he saw in the couple before him was what he and Olivia had promised themselves they would have at their age. Love, respect, and comfort. Instead, however, he was faced with accusations, betrayal, and shattered dreams. He wished he could turn back the clock, to relive the past few years and see if it was indeed him who had pushed her away.

"More tea, officers?" Mrs. Williams asked, offering them a weary smile.

"Thank you very much, but no. You have both been extremely helpful, but we must be on our way."

Mr. Williams stood and offered his hand to each of the men in turn. He had an incredibly firm grip for a man of his age, and the look on Lewis' face made it appear as though Mr. Williams had squeezed a little too tight.

THE WIND BIT at the back of Graham's neck as they walked down the street towards the car, and he turned up the collar on his jacket to ease the sting. Since leaving the house, neither man had uttered a word to the other. They walked in silence, each in deep reflection.

Graham thought about the part of the city they found themselves in. A quiet suburb with immaculately manicured lawns and trimmed hedges. The cars parked on the driveways shone in what little light escaped between the clouds. Neighbours greeted each other with honest smiles and the ground was clean and free of litter. An area not too dissimilar from where he had called home as recently as a year ago. An area that was in stark contrast to where he now put his head down at night. That was a street that was decorated with torn couches and soiled mattresses. The ground defiled with dog faeces, discarded needles, and old washing machines. A place he longed to be free of. A place he felt he did not belong.

Lewis was the first to speak, and his voice cut through the silence like a hot knife through soft butter.

"So ... what do you think?" he asked wearily.

Graham leaned up against the bonnet of his Jeep and took a cigarette from his jacket pocket. He closed his eyes and inhaled deeply.

What do I think?

When he eventually opened them, the look he gave his partner, his closest friend, was one of fear and bitter disappointment. He said nothing as he took his phone from the inside of his jacket.

"Morgan, it's me," he said bluntly. "You're not going to like this."

8

SEPTEMBER 17TH 2018, 11:04

STEAM BELLOWED into the air as the kettle on the stove whistled. Jackson took the cast-iron pot by the handle, his hand guarded by a tea towel, and poured the boiling water into the tall, glass tea pot. He was making his favourite brew. Golden Ceylon. A specialty of Sri Lanka.

Elena. Elena Robinson.

He had thought of little else since their first encounter the night before. The memory of those eyes had occupied his mind. That sweet laugh and wit. And *that* body. She had consumed his every waking moment. Much to his surprise and utter delight, he stood now, in his dimly lit kitchen, making tea, arranging to see her again.

The lighting was not because of homely neglect or a lack of windows. Quite the opposite, in fact. The space that Jackson called home, his refuge, his Mecca, was a sight to behold. A top-floor apartment with exceptional views over the bay from its enclosed balcony. Lavishly furnished with hardwood floors, exposed brickwork, and ornate mood lighting. The kitchen was bespoke, hand crafted, as were the ceiling-height bookshelves that flanked it. Full height windows ran the width of the home and provided unrivalled natural light and an enviable panorama of the ocean. It was not a television, but a vintage-style record player that took centre stage in the lounge. Positioned in such a way that the music would filter to all corners of the home. Filling the space with the works of Newton Faulkner, Xavier Rudd and John Butler, among others. It was one of the few places in the world that Jackson Page felt safe, felt that he could let the mask slip and be himself.

Communication between the pair had started almost as soon as Jackson had left the book launch. It all started with a simple message.

It's me, the illustrator x.

The conversation flowed effortlessly, with messages back and forth. Texts, picture messages, jokes and even a phone call that lasted into the early hours. Much to both of their joy, they had many things in common. From books and music, to more poignant topics, such as the way they viewed the world, and what they each felt was wrong with society. Jackson had much to say on that subject.

To help matters along, Jackson had taken out a sort of insurance policy. The more he knew about her, the better he could bend his answers in a more favourable direction. Knowledge was power.

Jackson was not on social media, but James was. An alter ego he'd created, complete with a stock profile photo from the internet, that he could use to view and digest the online lives of the people around him.

It is always better to be one step ahead.

As it happened, Elena's online life was not all me, me,

me like a lot of girls her age. It was deeper than that. Sure, she posted selfies, nothing too candid, however, good enough for Jackson to keep himself entertained in the evening away from the prying eyes of the world, but there was *more* to her.

Photography was her life. *Capturing emotion*, as she put it. Her skills behind the lens were impressive, no doubt, and the way in which she intertwined story into her compositions left Jackson in awe.

A true artist, he thought.

From his perspective, at least, it appeared the affection was mutual. She told him she thought he was funny and attractive. She had been complimentary about his work as well, which had only inflated his ego further and given him the confidence to ask her out on a date. She had said yes, as he hoped she would, and they arranged to meet for dinner the coming Friday evening.

THE ADRENALINE RAN through him like boiled water through a pipe. The hairs on the back of his neck stood on end and he started sweating. There was never meant to be a second, let alone a third. She stared up at him from the lock screen of his phone, and his breathing deepened.

I wasn't looking for you, so why, how, did you find me? he thought, his mind racing. His hands were getting clammy now, too.

He moved unconsciously into the bedroom, not for one second taking his gaze from his screen as he knelt beside the bed. He reached under and removed a section of floor board, exposing a small wooden box with a hinged lid. The box was old and worn and he sat it down in front of him. He lifted the lid and stared down at the contents below. Two phones. He clicked them both on and looked at the two smiling faces now glaring back at him. His girls. His *special* girls. Girls who fitted his criteria perfectly. Girls he had not searched for, but who had found him by chance when he was at his hungriest. Girls he felt that fate had handed to him on a silver platter. He returned his gaze to the phone in his hand, unsure if she would join them. Whether they needed the company. Whether *he* needed the company.

JACKSON THUMBED the screen of his phone while taking a sip of his tea. He wanted to catch up on the day's news before heading out, and a particular headline caught his attention.

Police update on murdered girls.

He clicked the link. Most of it was legal waffle, and it seemed that the police had now linked the recent killing to one from almost a year ago. There were some heartwarming comments from the parents and friends of the deceased as well.

Touching, Jackson thought, putting his empty cup in the sink.

The police, it seemed, were trying their best to reassure the public of their safety. That they were doing all they could to protect them and hunt down the monster. They gave out some brilliant advice too.

"Don't walk alone at night, carry a whistle, let someone know where you are."

What do they think I am? Jackson chuckled.

At the bottom of the article, there was a video. An interview with a police officer. A man named *Detective Inspector Graham Walker.* A passionate speaker, Jackson noted, a man with fire in his eyes and authority in his voice.

"Whoever you are, we will find you," the officer said at the end of the video, staring front-on into the camera.

Jackson smiled to himself, putting on his jacket as he walked towards the door.

"BEST OF LUCK, DETECTIVE," he said aloud, as he pulled the door behind him and walked towards his car. "I look forward to it."

9

"ALRIGHT, ALRIGHT YOU LOT, SETTLE DOWN," DCI Morgan said, taking off his coat. "I would like for us not to be here until tea time, and we have more than a few things to cover."

The chattering amongst the officers quietened down and everyone turned their focus to the two photographs stuck to the whiteboard at the front of the room. Graham was there, as was Lewis, front, and centre, eager to get started. Graham was biting the nail of his thumb in anticipation. He had not been sleeping well, and the bags under his eyes showed it.

Morgan continued, "As I am sure you are now all aware, there is a possible link between the killings of the two young women pictured behind me."

A few of the people present exchanged looks of uncertainty, although they all remained quiet. More than a few of the detectives in the department were sceptical, and many believed the similarities in the killings to be nothing more than an unfortunate coincidence. Something they kept between themselves, to avoid the wrath of the man now addressing them. Lewis tapped the end of his pen against his teeth, much to the aggravation of Graham, who took the pen from him and threw it on the ground, shaking his head.

"We believe a single person or persons is responsible. And it would be naïve of us to assume that they will not kill again."

There was a collective gasp, and several arms shot up around the room.

"What do we know about the mask?" one voice said.

"Any idea when, boss?" said another.

Graham turned on his seat and shot one man a cold stare, visibly stunned by his apparent stupidity. A chunky man, with curly dark hair, streaked with grey and choked with far too much gel. Although clearly younger than Graham, his weight and choice in attire made him appear much older.

"It doesn't work like that, Andrews," he said calmly. "These people, unfortunately for us, do not run on schedules. There was nearly a year between Sophie and Jessica. So, it could be a year, a month, or a day. And for all we know, he could dress the next body up like a fucking performing clown doing cartwheels." Graham turned back to face front, and Andrews receded in his chair, clearly embarrassed.

"Thank you, Detective Inspector Walker," Morgan said with an uncharacteristic grin. "Now, we don't have a lot to go on apart from the girls' physical similarities and the locations of their disposal. The mask is new. But that doesn't mean that whoever is responsible is not playing around with how they like to do things. Our only angle at the moment is the car. Now, there could be a few thousand dark estate cars in the city. So I'll be splitting a few of you into teams. I'll need you to cross reference cars with that description, with people who have previous. That should narrow our pool of suspects to begin with." Groans erupted from around the room.

"Yes, it's a long shot, but it's what we have, and it's what you lot get bloody paid for."

Morgan turned to Graham and Lewis, his face a wonderful shade of tomato that morning, glistening with beads of sweat that ran the length of his forehead.

"Go and see Jessica's parents, and have a sniff about at her uni house, see if we can learn something that way."

Both men nodded in quiet agreement.

"The rest of you, I want you checking through the girls' social media accounts, talking to friends, work colleagues, anything we can to see if there is some other link between them both."

Sounds of, "Yes boss" and, "Alright Guv" echoed around the room, like the world's least in-tune and in-time acapella group. Everyone in that room knew what was at stake. If the theories were correct, then the killer, or killers, were only one victim away from "serial" status, something nobody in that room wanted looming over them. The media would have a field day and make all of their jobs that much more difficult. Despite the groans, there was a combined sense of purpose in the briefing room that morning. All officers present, focused on a single, unifying goal.

"HAVE YOU GOT THEIR ADDRESS?" Graham asked as Lewis approached the car.

He leaned against the front wing of his Jeep, cigarette between his lips, reading a copy of the pathology report that Ainsley had been kind enough to email over.

"Yeah, I've got it, and Jessica's address in Cathays."

"Brilliant, at least now we haven't got to faff about in the morning."

"Fancy a swift one?"

He inhaled the rest of his cigarette and threw the butt to the ground. The smile escaping from his lips said 'yes' but his eyes, those deep blue pools of exhaustion and pain, they said 'no, please let me sleep'.

"AYE GO ON THEN. Just the one though."

10

Jackson Page gazed upon a body. His own body. From the perspective of a free-standing, full-length mirror that dominated the corner of his bedroom. The figure now standing before him, still glistening with droplets of water from the shower, bore the tone of a professional athlete, and was testament to a lifestyle dedicated to personal well-being.

That night was going to be special, and he wished to look his best. Personal preparations had begun an hour prior. Careful selection of that evening's outfit (a slim-fitting, long-sleeved white shirt, paired with a pair of tight-fitting brown corduroys and complemented by a pair of well-worn loafers) was accompanied by the graceful sounds of Newton Faulkner, spinning on the record player in the other room.

He'd taken the time to shave. A subtle rebellion against the raging tide of the heavily bearded of late. A ritual that always preceded the day's bathing. He preferred to shave the classic way. Straight razor. A process as old as shaving itself.

A process that began with preparing the skin, using hot water to open the pores and soften the face. Soap, applied by brush, generously lathered over the area, and the moisture that condensed upon the bathroom mirror, wiped away. His razor of choice was an antique piece of unknown origin, constructed from an oiled teak handle and a polished steel blade. A blade that, despite regular sharpening and maintenance, was tarnishing with age. Experience had taught him that the hold was key. Hold the blade too flat, and it will tear the stubble. If held too steep, it will cut the skin and ruin the finish.

JACKSON TURNED from the mirror and walked towards the bed, towel drying his brown, shoulder-length hair as he went. His phone, resting upon the outfit which he had carefully laid out on the bed, vibrated. He typed in the password with an almost mechanical efficiency and peered down at the screen.

I'm really looking forward to tonight, Elena x, the message read.

He exhaled deeply through his nose, as the beginning of a smirk began to creep from the corner of his mouth. Sweeping his hair back with his one free hand, he shot a glance at the clock that hung on the wall above the bed.

As am I, he began his reply, *See you at eight...*

Every cell in his body was on fire. Adrenaline flowed through his very core and powered his every movement at the thought of her. Elena. *His* Elena.

How will tonight end? he thought. *Will I indulge? Will I have my dessert?*

Jackson tied his damp hair into a loose topknot and made his way into the living room. As he lifted the needle from the record player, he glimpsed himself in the window, and smiled back at the twisted, ghostly reflection.

Phone. Keys. Wallet. *And something else.*

Leaving now, see you soon. He pressed send as he reached for the handle, the brisk evening air kissing his face as the door opened into the night, and he took a step towards *her.*

SHE LOOKED RADIANT, standing outside the restaurant waiting for him to arrive. The blue of her denim dress complemented the blonde of her hair perfectly, and it sat just below her knees, leaving her chunky black boots exposed and the tattoos that adorned her shins free to breathe in the brisk evening air. Her smile lit up the entire street when she spotted him.

"Hi, you," she said with a nervous grin.

See, I told you I wasn't lying. I told you she was a beauty.

She held her left elbow with the opposing hand, making her stance edgy to any onlookers. And she gave him a small, anxious wave.

"Hi yourself."

His voiced oozed a calm confidence that he did not have the last time they met. And he *felt* confident, despite the battle raging within.

Jackson handed her a single, coral-coloured tulip he had been hiding behind his back. And her face lit up as she took the flower to her nose and inhaled.

"Quite the gentleman," she jested.

She looked up at him from beneath long, dark lashes. He thought that her green eyes were intoxicating, as she threw him a look that was laced with self-assertive lust. His heart fluttered. And under his crisp, white shirt, he began to sweat. He swallowed hard, trying to stem his nerves before offering her his hand.

"Shall we?" he said.

THE RESTAURANT WAS DIMLY LIT, and the air was heavy with the scent of candles and spiced food. The tables, positioned close together, were dressed in traditional Mexican decoration, each with its own glass-surrounded tea-light and a carafe of still water.

The restaurant was not furnished in an ungainly fashion, like many of the popular South American-themed chains. Those, Jackson felt, were guilty of a number of societal sins, ranging from thinly disguised cultural appropriation to overt racism. All conveniently available wrapped in a soft flour tortilla, and yours for only ten pounds, ninety-nine. Soft drink included.

He reached over the table and took her hand in his, gazing into the deep, green pools of her eyes. He slowed his breathing to speak. And when he opened his mouth, his voice was barely a whisper.

"You look incredible this evening," he said, playing with her fingers.

She looked away for a second and blushed.

"So, is that your game?" Elena asked, throwing him a cheeky smirk as she brushed the fringe from her eyes.

"I'm sorry?"

"The eighteenth-century gentleman routine. Is that how you're planning to get into my underwear?"

"I wasn't... I mean, I'm not..." he stuttered.

"I'm fucking with you dude, relax." She burst into a fit of laughter.

Surprise ran across Jackson's face. But, after a moment of

panic, he joined her, laughing. He thought her sense of humour was refreshing, and it made him feel immediately at ease in her presence. And although his attraction to her was growing by the second, the itch, his itch, still gnawed away in the back of his mind.

The waiter arrived at their table. Elena ordered a Pina Colada, while Jackson poured himself a glass from the tepid jug of table water. The conversation was effortless. As it had been by phone. And Jackson found himself transfixed, even hypnotised by her. Even the smallest of details, such as the way she played with her straw as she spoke, or fixed her eyes on his, sent bursts of adrenaline through his entire body. He had never felt like this before. Not anywhere close to this, in fact. And that scared him.

"I am going to powder my nose, sir," she said, chuckling sweetly as the waiter took the last of the plates from their table.

Elena got up from her seat and moved with all the majesty of a white swan on a still pond. She floated towards the ladies' room, throwing him a smile over her shoulder before disappearing beyond its threshold.

If she was going to join them, *his* girls, now was his chance. He reached into the pocket of his trousers. His breathing was elevating and his heart began pounding in his ears. And from his pocket, he withdrew a tiny vial of white powder. He held it in his hand, carefully hiding it from view.

How much do I want you? How much do I need you?

'Helper', as it had become known in certain circles, was a synthetic anaesthetic. And it had become available for purchase from some of the less genteel corners of the internet. A powerful drug that dissolved in fluids and, at present, did not show up on any police toxicology reports. It was Rohypnol for the modern, discerning monster.

Jackson paused. He thought for a long moment, playing with the vial, moving it between his sweating fingers. He wanted her. Wanted her for himself. But not in the same way as the others, not this time. What he was feeling for her, for Elena, was new and alien, and it made absolutely no sense to him. It scared the hell out of him, in truth. He wanted to *be* with her. To hear her laugh. To touch the soft skin of her hands and embrace her. To protect her. To love her. He took a napkin from the table and dabbed his brow. His hands shook.

What is this fresh hell?

She re-appeared from beyond the door of the toilet and began making her way back towards their table. He shot her a wide smile from across the room as he slipped the vial quietly back into his pocket.

NOT THIS TIME, he thought. *You are mine. My Elena.*

11

———

JANUARY, 1997

THE BOY with the blue backpack slid himself under the slats of his metal framed bed, putting his gloved hands tight to his ears. He could hide here. Hide from the noise.

Mum was crying again. Sobbing, howling like a banshee, and Dad was shouting. He had been all evening since returning home from the pub or wherever he had been. It was not all screaming and shouting though. In the interim, there was the crash and bang of thrown plates and furniture, bowls and vases. Dad had punched a hole in a door tonight; that was new. His own private, live action soap opera, airing every night. He was even a special guest in some episodes. In tonight's incredibly special episode. Tonight, his life would change forever.

THE SCREAMING and shouting were getting louder. The bangs and crashes, more frequent. He hoped it would end soon. Tears were running down his cheek, leaving a damp patch on the carpet below and a salty taste in his mouth. There was one final colossal bang, a deathly scream. Then silence. He heard footsteps on the kitchen tile moving towards the door. The door opened, then closed again. And then there was only silence.

12

SEPTEMBER 18TH 2018, 10.30

THAT MORNING HAD NOT BEEN a complete failure, apart from the flat tyre and a coffee-stained shirt. Graham and Lewis had learned something from Jessica's parents. The meeting had not been an easy one, as they had expected. Between the sniffles and sobs of the grieving parents, they had learned that their daughter had been speaking to, and had arranged to meet, a new man. Unfortunately for Graham, however, they knew nothing about him, not even a name. As it so happened, Jessica had been hesitant to share many personal details of her life with her parents, who were devout Christians, and none too pleased with the party life-style many students adopted, their daughter included. The countless crosses that had adorned their home made Graham uneasy, and he was more than happy to leave as soon as was polite.

Jessica's phone, along with many other of her posses-sions, had never been recovered, and that made tracing her last movements that much harder. Graham had his fingers crossed that Jessica's housemates could shed some light on her last days, or new man. He parked the car down the street from the address, the driver's door complaining with an audible creak as he got out and turned his cheek into the crisp, morning air. He looked at the car and patted it gently on the bonnet, his own body mirroring the sentiment.

Like so many streets in this part of the city, the vast majority of houses there were now student lets. Trophies from hard nights of partying decorated the walled-in front areas of the scarcely maintained houses. The locals were not best pleased, as one could expect. Although that was not just down to the litter and noise. There was big money to be made in renting these homes out and, as a result, local house prices were being pushed sky high from outside investment, beyond the reach of many who had been born there.

"Number fifty-eight, Gray. Just up there." Lewis pointed, his hand clutching a piece of paper, to a house with a blue, vintage-style bike with a wicker basket, leaning against the front wall.

"Jesus, it looks like a bloody crack-house," Graham said, laughing to himself as they approached the door. A door that he noted could have done with a good lick of paint and a thorough clean.

The girl who answered looked like she had just rolled out of bed. It was just past two in the afternoon. Her brown, chest-length hair hung in unbrushed mats to one side, and was sparsely dotted with glitter, Graham guessed, from the night before. Or the night before that, perhaps. She wore thick-framed black glasses that did nothing to cover the face of someone nursing a colossal hangover. He knew the feeling well. Christ, he was experiencing much of the same himself, and he sympathised.

"Yeah?" she barked, almost swinging the door from its hinges.

"Detectives Walker and Reed, South Wales Police," Lewis said, holding out his warrant card.

"Fuckin' ell," she replied, guarding her eyes from the low, autumn sun. "About Jessie, is it? You had better come in."

Graham soon wished he were back with the crosses of the Evans household. The smell of instant noodles and stale alcohol hit him as soon as he entered. The door slammed behind them, and the girl kicked empty beer cans and a pizza box out of the way as she showed them to what he assumed was a kitchen. For all he knew, it could have been a public amenity site. Rubbish and dirty dishes covered the entirety of the worktops, and the sink was overflowing with days old water. Parts of someone's leftover meal floated happily along, between cups, plates, and bowls. And a number of flies had gathered for the after party.

"Fag?" the girl asked, pulling a crumpled packet of cigarettes from her food-stained dressing gown. She offered one to each of the detectives in turn, one hanging from her own dried and chapped lips.

"No, I'm fine, thanks," Lewis replied.

Graham simply held his hand up and shook his head. She shrugged and continued to light hers. The smoke rose from the lit cigarette and climbed towards the already stained ceiling, adding to the eclectic assortment of smells that originated from the kitchen.

"Anyway, Miss..." Graham started.

"Harriet," she said, cutting across him.

"Harriet, what can you tell us about Miss Evans?"

"Not much like," she took a long draw on her cigarette and exhaled. "She was a nice girl, she kept herself to herself. She did like a drink, though. Like all of us, I guess. She always got a bit lairy after a few, did our Jessie."

"Any boyfriends?" Lewis asked.

"She'd bring a few lads back here and shag 'em, but you couldn't call them boyfriends, really," she said with a smirk.

Harriet threw the spent cigarette into the sink and took a sip from her teacup. "The last night we saw her though, some guy did pick her up for a date."

Graham's ears pricked up, and he leaned forward.

"Dunno who he was. She had met him recently, didn't have a photo, though, which was odd, to show us if he was fit like. Don't think he had socials or something."

"Do you mean he didn't use social media?" Graham asked.

"Yep. Who doesn't these days? Weirdo."

The two men looked at each other, knowing that neither one of them did. They were from the old school. Love letters, mix tapes and phone calls, instead of pokes and dick pics. Graham could not think of anything worse than spending your life glued to a screen, head down, neck bent like a chicken ready for the Sunday roast, avoiding at all cost real social interaction.

"Did you by any chance see what car he was driving?" Lewis asked.

Harriet brushed the ash from the front of her dressing gown and lit another cigarette.

"Some big posh thing," she replied, shrugging.

"A Volvo?"

"Yeah, suppose it could have been, not too sure. It was smart, though."

Lewis finished writing his notes and then lifted his head, seeing the intrigue and concern on his partner's face.

"Thanks," Graham said. "If we need anything else, one of us will give you a shout. We're going to go up and have a look in Jessica's room, if that's okay?"

"No worries, you guys crack on. I'm going back to bed," she replied.

With mug and a fresh cigarette in hand, she walked out of the kitchen, back towards the front door, and went into the first door on the left. She turned and looked at the pair, as tears started collecting in her eyes.

"Just do me a favour, yeah? Catch this sick fuck, for Jessie. She didn't deserve this." Harriet shook her head, visibly holding back floods, and closed the door behind her.

CONSIDERING the state on the ground floor of the house, Jessica's room, on the first floor, was nothing like what the pair had expected. It was neatly laid out and immaculately clean, files and textbooks stacked methodically on the desk. The bed was made, and dirty dishes and soiled underwear were nowhere to be seen.

Lewis was uneasy being in a teenage girl's room. He felt as though he were trespassing, invading her personal space. This did not seem to bother Graham, who had already donned blue latex gloves and was searching through drawers at quite a pace. It looked like he was searching for drugs, or guns, or some other hot contraband.

"She was a careful girl in some regards, at least," Graham said, holding a half-empty packet of condoms.

"Jesus, Gray, have a little class, mate."

Graham smiled. "Of all the sick shit we've seen together

– bodies, car wrecks – a used packet of johnnies gets you going."

Lewis said nothing, he just shook his head and continued searching.

THEY FOUND nothing of use to them or the case. That was, unless archived fashion magazines and vintage records were any good at bringing down killers. Annoyed and disheartened, Graham sat on the bed, took off his gloves and threw them into the wastepaper basket. He took his phone in his hand, slid it open and looked up at Lewis, defeated.

"We need to find that bloody car," he snapped. "And soon."

Standing up, Graham walked over to the window and looked out into the grim street below. The lane behind the uni house was full of rubbish and disused furniture, much like the street he was living in.

What the fuck is wrong with people?

INHALING DEEPLY, allowing the disappointment to disperse into the air, he looked down to his phone and dialled.

13

THERE WAS NO SWEETER sound to Graham's ears than liquid running over ice. It numbed the pain, the anguish, the disappointment of the day and drowned out the sounds of the night. The sounds of unsettled domestic life, substance abuse and missed opportunities that came from the other side of his front door. Sounds of the underbelly, the darker side of the city. Sounds that had recently become home.

It was not the loneliness that bothered him. In fact, the time to reflect was a godsend compared to the constant bustle of the office. It was the unfamiliarity, and the lack of a comfortable routine, that had really become a problem once he was on his own. He had found it difficult to adjust, to come to terms with his new normal. His new reality.

In days gone by, he would have returned from work to a warm home and open arms. Conversation about the day's happenings and a family meal around the dining table. His only companions now came in bottles and cans and gave you a splitting headache after a while if you let them stay long enough. That's not to say it was a one-sided relationship. They helped him forget sometimes, to relax and feel almost normal. Sometimes he spiralled, however, and there had been more than one occasion when he had found himself on top of a bridge, bottle in hand, considering whether to end it all. The only thing that had kept him from tumbling, from welcoming the great abyss, was *her*.

HE SAT that night with whisky on the rocks and his back to the wall. He had not bothered to furnish the house apart from the absolute necessities. Only a television and an ashtray in the living room, no couch, cushions or rugs. His hair still dripped wet from the shower.

The television was on, not that he was watching it. It was background noise to stop him going insane and to mask some of the moaning of Sharon from next door. They were getting on tonight, it seemed. The microwave pinged, curry for one. A statement that by itself was depressing.

His doctor, a man who Graham had little faith in, a man who appeared to be older than time itself, had prescribed him pills to help. To help him sleep. To help him smile through the day as if nothing were wrong. To help him function as a man.

What harm could they do? he thought, washing them down. The whisky, it seemed, did not complement the taste of a microwave korma that well.

He thought of calling Ainsley, to tell her how he felt, that he felt the same. She was wonderful, a real catch. But what self-respecting woman would want a grieving mess of a man, a man who struggled to dress himself most mornings. What could he offer her besides disappointment? He thought better of it and put his phone down; it crashed to the floor as it slipped from his intoxicated fingers.

She really is beautiful, he thought, pouring himself another drink.

THE GLASSES CAME AND WENT. The bottle came and went. And Graham Walker ended the night slumped on the bare floor of his home, drink in hand, alone.

14

THE LATE MORNING sun shone through the aged, stained curtains and disturbed Graham's sleep. He fidgeted on the bare wooden floor, his hand landing in last night's dinner. His phone, now with a newly smashed screen, lay a foot from his head. It vibrated loudly on the floor, and he shot up.

"Fuck me," he said, clearly startled.

He guarded his eyes from the incoming light and reached around for the vibrating mobile. His hand knocked over a glass, and the remaining alcohol drifted along the floor to join up with the congealed orange mess that had dripped from the microwavable container. He wiped the sleep from his eyes and stared down at the now barely legible screen.

4 Missed Calls – Reed.

Incoming Call – Office.

"Oh, Jesus H Christ," he said under his breath, cradling his thumping head.

Taking a deep, laboured breath, he answered the call.

"Gray, Morgan is losing his shit," Lewis said in a hushed tone. "Splash some water on your face and get yourself down here."

"Lewis, I'm on my way," Graham said with a groan. He covered his mouth with a hand, trying not to vomit.

"If I were you, I would bring the man some flowers, or bring a tub of Vaseline, your choice."

The line went dead.

Graham lay back down and stared up at the ceiling. It was spinning. The taste in his mouth, the taste of cheap whisky and tobacco, was overpowering, and it sickened him. It made him feel like a failure. He wished he had not woken up.

THE OFFICERS in Graham's department called it "The Bull Pen". An arrangement of old wooden desks, squeezed together and covered in computers, telephones, piles of paperwork and stained coffee mugs. The noise was almost always deafening. Between the phones ringing off the hook and detectives shouting back and forth, it was a wonder how they worked with so little room to think. But they made breakthroughs there. Cases were broken and careers were made. Ordinary men and women turned into momentary superheroes and local celebrities when the big fish were brought down, and when the monsters were pulled from the shadows and brought to justice. Graham was not so optimistic that morning, however, and he found the noise to be almost crippling.

He slumped at his desk and took a long draw from the

disposable coffee cup in his hand. He looked over to Lewis, who worked directly opposite him, and through the ever-darkening bags of his eyes, he smiled apologetically.

"Lewis, I messed up," he said sincerely, holding his hand in the air.

"You haven't got to explain yourself to me, mate. You know that. Your liver and Morgan, on the other hand, are a different story."

Lewis had always been patient with him. He did not know why and never asked. Lewis Reed was a good man. He would always try to see through someone's darkness to the light within. Graham thought that Lewis would have given Satan himself a second chance at redemption, and he hated letting his friend down. He had been doing so a lot recently.

DCI Morgan's receptionist, Emma, popped her head around the door of the Bull Pen and motioned to Graham. A sweet woman in her early thirties, who he hoped was not being taken advantage of by her boss; Morgan had a reputation for seducing women in the workplace, and it had almost cost him his job more than once. Graham thought she looked stronger than the others, however, and he hoped she was.

"Walker, he wants to see you," she said, smiling nervously.

He smiled back. "Thanks Emma. I'm on my way."

He stood up, fixed his jacket, and finished the rest of his coffee in a single gulp, throwing the empty cup into the bin.

"How do I look, Lew, honestly?"

"Like shit," Lewis said with a grin. "Just try not to look him in the eye."

.   .   .

GRAHAM PUSHED THE DOOR AJAR, just enough so that he could squeeze his head past the frame and not expose his entire body to the wrath of Morgan. Morgan had his back turned. He was looking out of the window of his office, his hands clutched and held behind his back.

"Come in, Graham, shut the door," he commanded. His voice was low but stern.

Morgan turned as Graham took a seat, planting his large, hair-covered hands on the desk. The look on his face shocked Graham. It was not a look of anger or disappointment, but that of deep-rooted concern and care. And it took him by surprise.

"Grayo, I know what you're going through, mate. And I know it's complete shit," he said, sitting down. "What that cow did was unforgivable, but you cannot keep letting her take things from you."

"Sir?"

"You and I both know you are killing yourself, drowning yourself in that crap. For Christ's sake, I can smell it on you now."

Graham looked down at his feet. This was not the man he wanted to be. He was like a schoolboy again in the headmaster's office. He was a well-respected police officer, spiralling into oblivion, with his career on a knife's edge. He could feel it trying to pull him under, and it was winning. He was struggling for breath.

"Sir," he said, nodding in humiliation.

"Let us help you. Let *me* help you. There's a fantastic group in town. They've helped out a few people here over the years. Let me reach out for you."

Graham was hesitant to respond, and he paused for a long moment. He'd started to sweat, and he could swear he could smell the booze leaking from his pores. It made him feel nauseous, and the office spun.

Me, in rehab?

"Graham, I won't lie to you, you're on thin ice, mate." Morgan's voice had turned suddenly cold. "This is your last chance. Take our help, get your shit together, or you'll be working security down the local supermarket, and no one, me included, wants to see that."

Graham lifted his head and took a deep breath to stem the rising bile. He swallowed hard and extended a clammy hand to Morgan.

"THANKS, MATE," he said, his voice almost a whisper. "I appreciate your concern. I'll... I'll do it."

15

THE PAIR WALKED hand in hand, beaming at each other. It was surprisingly pleasant for the time of year, and Cardiff's Bute Park was alive with activity. Groups ran together through the trees, children kicked balls to and fro on the grass. Elderly couples, holding each other tight for stability, threw bread and seeds into the pond, hoping to attract the ducks and swans that floated with majesty on the calm, blue waters.

They had only known each other for a short time, but to the outside world they appeared madly in love. Their body language and facial expressions did nothing to hide the growing admiration between the pair. Jackson held on his right arm, Elena. *His* Elena. His left hand carried a basket, laden with wine and fine food that he had assembled himself to delight her. They stopped under the shade of an old sycamore tree and laid out the blanket that he had strewn across the wicker-work box.

The early autumnal sun filtered through the remaining leaves and cast an amber glow on the soft lines of on her face. A stray leaf, caught in the breeze, landed on top of her head and got caught in her golden, flowing hair. He leaned in, removed it with the gentlest of movements, laid it in her palm, and kissed her.

She opened her eyes and looked up at him from underneath her long, dark lashes.

"This is a very welcome treat," she said.

"How do you mean?" he asked, brushing a strand of stray hair from her face.

"Let's just say you're not like a lot of guys I've known."

He chuckled. "Knowing some lads around here, I'll take that as a compliment." He imagined Joel, ass-grabbing his way through the office every morning, happy knowing that she had not immediately pigeonholed him along with the rest of them.

"Honestly though," she continued. "Where did you come from? What is *your* story?"

"That, my lady, would take far too long to explain." He took a bottle and a glass from the basket, uncorking the wine as he spoke. "And besides, I'm far more interested in you. I would love to get to know the *real* Elena."

"Alright then, mister. You can keep your secrets, for now," she said with a laugh and a flirtatious look, holding the glass as Jackson filled it. "None for you?"

"Not today," he replied, smiling.

She started at the beginning, where she was born, her first years in school, her first broken bone, her first kiss. Jackson sat in quiet admiration, more than happy just to listen, just to be in her presence, to watch her body flow as she moved between topics. She spoke with passion. He thought her voice was like the sweetest music to his ears. He was intoxicated, obsessed, with her. And his fingers clenched the blanket tighter and tighter the more she spoke. She didn't take her eyes from his.

She only looks at me; only has eyes for me.

"What about your parents?"

"Oh god." She groaned, draining the glass. "Now that is a long story. A bloody messy one at that." He leaned in and kissed her gently on the forehead.

"Amuse me."

"Well," she started, "I won't bore you with the details. Mum is passionate. She is an artist, in every sense of the word, but she craves attention. And my dad works, a lot, and drinks a little too much."

Her face grew sombre as she recalled the details.

"Basically, it was never going to work. They had me, stuck together for that reason, I guess and then it all fell apart. No, sorry, it all came crashing down. They must have loved each other at some point. I'm sure Dad still loves her even now."

Tears gathered in her eyes, and she played with the stalk of the glass, looking at the ground.

"But hey, no one died, they broke up and now I'm stuck in the middle, cleaning up their mess."

"I'm sorry," Jackson said, taking her hand in his.

"Don't worry," she scoffed. "First world problems and all that."

She wiped the tears from her eyes and smiled at him. He loved her honesty, her outlook. He loved that beneath her witty exterior, was a sweet, caring, *real* person. He felt as though he could almost trust her. *Almost.*

Trust was not something that came easily to Jackson. It had been shattered far too many times before. There was something here, though, something with her. It made him want to offer his trust to her, to give it to her freely. It was as though she was incapable of hurting him, somehow, and that scared and excited him in equal measures. She sucked him in.

AFTER INDULGING in Jackson's exquisite spread – plant-based, of course – the pair lay under the ageing sycamore, talking, and laughing, until the sun was low in the September sky. He accompanied her, walking hand in hand, to the entrance of the park, where her taxi was waiting.

"I've had a great time today," she said, floating silently beside him.

Jackson was not a short man by any means, and Elena was not the tallest of girls, but she had no trouble keeping up. Her long, slender legs easily kept pace with his.

As they approached the entrance to the park, the taxi sat patiently on the road opposite. Jackson stopped and turned to face her, clasping his hands together at the base of her back.

"Do I get the pleasure of your company tomorrow?" he asked, kissing her passionately.

"Not tomorrow, Casanova," she replied, smiling and pushing him away playfully. "I have to go and see my dad. Check in on him. He's a little fragile these days, and he hasn't been returning my calls, or my texts, which is a worry."

"I'd like to meet him."

"Steady on," she said, laughing. "Next, you'll be down on one knee, and I'll be pregnant."

She held her hand underneath her belly and pushed out. She looked up at him and burst into a fit of laughter. A moment of panic crossed his face, pushing her to laugh harder.

The car across the road sounded its horn, and she turned to him, pecking him on the cheek.

"I'll text you later," she said as she walked away. "Thanks again, for today."

I WILL SEE YOU TOMORROW, my love, he thought, waving her off. *But you will not see me.*

16

1986

THE BELL RANG as the day's final lesson ended. A herd of bodies rushed towards the buses, like a stampede with backpacks, powered by raging hormones. He spied her through the crowd and gave a wave. Her friends all giggled behind cupped hands, but she didn't care. She waved back, beaming in his direction. They were going to the end of school prom together and she did not care who knew it. She had already bought her dress, and he, his suit.

He pinned a flower to her dress as they entered the grand hall of the hotel arm in arm. Her violet gown flowed elegantly as they danced. He took her, hands shaking and sweating, and pulled her close. He kissed her there, in front of everyone. She was his, and he wanted them to know it.

1992

. . .

THE CROWD WAS ONLY SMALL, but it roared with admiration and excitement as he took the stage and shook hands with the speaker. He looked so handsome in his new uniform, she thought, and she could not have been prouder of her man.

They moved together and worked the crowd. He introduced her – his voice full of love – to everyone he could.

Look who I am with, he thought. *How lucky am I?*

He took her by the hand and pulled her close. He kissed her there, in front of everyone. She was his, and he wanted them to know it.

1993

THE HIGH SUMMER day was hot, and the sun beamed down from a cloudless sky. The air was humid and thick, and the mosquitoes bit at their skin as they walked. The trail was quiet, it was mid-week, and he had taken time off, especially for this day. The path wound left and right, up and down between the pines and oaks and streams. Sweat dripping from her brow, hair tied in a messy bun. He could not imagine a woman more beautiful.

They reached the top. The view over the valley, and over the woods beyond, was breathtaking. He reached into his pack and withdrew a bottle of champagne and two glasses, and sat them on the stump of a long dead tree.

He got down on one knee, pulled out a ring, and asked her to be his forever. Tears ran down her face as she accepted. He jumped up and pulled her close. He kissed her there, and she was his.

. . .

THE HOUSE WAS NOT much as it stood, but it was going to be a home. The paper was peeling, and the paint was flaking, but the couple stood in the lounge, paint brushes in hand, beaming.

They ripped up the carpets, they took out the doors, but day by day, week by week, they inched ever closer to turning their house into a home. More than once, they found each other flicking paint or painting lines on each other's clothes. They laughed, they shouted, they cried, and they smiled, but day by day, week by week, they inched ever closer to turning their house into a home.

As the rains of late November set in, they stood in their beautiful new kitchen, exhausted but content. He took her by the hand and pulled her close. He kissed her there, in their new home, and she was his.

1994

NINE MONTHS CAN GO by in a flash if you are not careful. They documented every step by photo and film. Unexpected yes, but a true blessing none the less. She was sick at first, every morning, and he was there to hold back her hair and rub her shoulders, to tell her how beautiful he thought she was.

Weeks became months, and his office, the spare room, was transformed into a magical place. The ceiling painted like the night sky and a rocking chair with a little bear sat waiting in the corner. The pair were excited beyond belief.

She held it well and worked until the very end. Her waters broke over a meal for two, their last, for quite some time. Twelve hours passed and two became three. He held her for the first time, looked down at his warrior of a wife, and through tears of joy, thanked her. He took her by the hand and the three of them stood close. He kissed each of them in turn, they were here, and they were his.

2010

GRAHAM NOW WORE a suit to work, and the days were getting longer too. No time for meals for two or a bath for three. She was alone, even though she was not.

When he was there, he was not. Drink became his friend, and he put all his trust in the bottle, opening up only after three or four. Opening up, only after all others had already gone to bed.

"It helps me sleep," he often said. "It helps me relax."

The weeks dragged into months, and they into years. Still, he would not stop, and he could not see the damage he was causing. She drifted further and further away.

He came home one night, late, and after the pub. He tried to take her by the hand, but she showed him the back of hers. He pulled her close, but she screamed. He kissed her there, but she was no longer his.

2017

TRUST HAD BROKEN DOWN, and they no longer knew one another. They were strangers, passing ships who shared a home. A home that was now just a house. Just four walls and memories.

Truth became lies, conversations became arguments, and inch by inch they drifted apart. She shut herself off, found the strength within to start anew with her daughter. He had never laid a finger on either of them. She knew there was a good man inside, still. But he was so caught up, so consumed by his own life, that he never saw what was happening underneath his own nose.

"She's staying with my mum," she often said. "I'm meeting the girls in town."

What made him eventually twig, to this day she did not know. Perhaps it was just that she had grown bored with trying to hide the new happiness she had found. He came home early one night. He must have skipped the pub or thought to try and catch her. Whatever the case, she imagined he saw more than he had bargained for.

He opened the front door and climbed the stairs silently. The house was in darkness. He looked left and his daughter's bedroom was empty, but there was someone here. He could hear them. He could smell them.

HE OPENED the door and screamed like a man possessed. She was being held close, and *he* was there, kissing her, and she, was no longer *his.*

17

HER DAY, Elena's day, always begins at around six thirty. She rises slowly, stretching, taking in the morning's first light with a sip of water. She checks her phone, sometimes texts me or a friend, and makes her way into her en-suite bathroom to wash up.

There is almost always yoga, and she looks so good in those tight shorts. Her bedroom window is large so I can see everything. But she cannot see me from here.

EVERY MORNING since that first meeting, Jackson had been braving the early morning cold to be with her. Her address had been easy to find, and she kept him company as he stood, coffee in hand, under a low-hanging tree across the street. The glare from the streetlight kept him silhouetted against the shadows, and the evergreen leaves kept away most of the weather. They were keeping each other company, and he was keeping her safe. He was always there if she needed him.

SHE LEAVES for work at around eight. She lives within walking distance of her office, and as long as I keep back, I can walk with her. We have breakfast together. She is a creature of habit, always the granola bowl and an oat latte from the same little café. I'll be honest, the coffee there is particularly good.

JACKSON ONLY WORKED around the corner, and some days they met up for lunch if she was not busy or on location. He loved those days; they were his favourite. In the interim, however, James would keep a watchful eye on her socials. To check how she was feeling, where she would be working if not in the office, who she was spending her time with. It was easier that way if he needed to bump into her, say, accidentally.

Life will be better for us both if I know everything about you and know where you are at all times.

ELENA'S JOB for that day was a fashion shoot she had landed for a local designer who was after an edgy take on their product photography. She had chosen the city centre as a backdrop to use some of the modern architecture to help accent her compositions. She felt as though the square lines and dramatic glass front of the buildings would provide a striking contrast to the bright, flamboyant nature of the designer's collection.

The shoot was going well, and about an hour in they

broke for lunch. And as if by an incredible stroke of fate, Jackson strode around the corner, right on cue.

"I know it's not a big city, but what are the chances?" he said, embracing her. "You look amazing."

She had to hold the camera high so that he didn't risk scratching the lens.

"I know, right," she replied with a raised eyebrow.

She looked happy, but behind her eyes there was a subtle hint of concern. "Jacks, you work, like, nowhere near here."

"Oh, I'm just meeting a friend for lunch in a café down the road." He motioned to a street behind her. "But now that you're here, maybe we can grab a bite?"

"I would love to, but I have to get back. Tomorrow maybe."

He looked over her shoulder, to the group of her colleagues all gathered together by their vans. And inside his stomach turned.

Male models? I bet they haven't taken their fucking eyes off of her.

"Yeah, sure, that sounds great," he said from behind gritted teeth. Inside, he was shaking. "Say hi to your dad from me."

"I'll be sure to do that. It's been nice to see you. I'll text you later."

Jackson was more than a little concerned at the direction she was walking in. This was not a nice area, that was well known. And it would be dark soon. She walked past a dilapidated corner shop, crossed the road, took a left and past a takeaway where a man catcalled from inside. But she took no notice.

It was lucky then, that even at this time of day, that this part of Cardiff was busy. There were enough sounds and smells, enough traffic on the road and people on the pavements that Jackson could easily melt into the crowd.

They passed a pub that, in days gone by, would have been the centre of this community. A place to meet after work and on the weekends and create memories with friends and family. Not now, though. A group were gathered by the door smoking. It was almost impossible to discern their age. Three men and a woman, who it seemed had been there since the early morning. They were staggering back and forth, shouting obscenities at passersby. One fell, face first, into the concrete. The others did little more than laugh.

Where the hell are you taking me? he thought, stepping over the drunk.

She came to a stop alongside a row of early sixties terrace houses. The houses closest to her had a large amount of white plastic patio furniture strewn about, broken into pieces. The house next door had a large trampoline and a paddling pool out front, and something was floating in the pool. A dead rat, perhaps. Or human waste.

She crossed the road and walked through a small, galvanised gate and up to the front door of one of the houses. This one seemed better maintained than the rest. A "to let" sign stood proudly in the middle of the uncut lawn and an old but clean four-by-four was parked out front.

Is this daddy?

He hid behind a corner, trying to control his breath as he watched on.

Elena tried the bell, but had no luck, so she rapped her hand on the door three times. She looked nervous, and she stood with the same anxious stance that she had when outside the restaurant, waiting for him.

A car carrying three teenage boys passed, its music blaring. One of them hung out of the window and threw something at the house across the street.

"That's what you get for fucking with us," he shouted.

The car sped off, narrowly missing the rear end of the four-wheel drive. A woman appeared from beyond the door, holding a baby and crying, shouting at the car as it disappeared into the night. Her faded nightdress blew about in the evening breeze, almost destroying her modesty.

Elena knocked on the door again. She took out her phone and held it to her ear. A light came on in the downstairs window and the door opened. She jumped at the man standing in the doorway and wrapped her arms around him, kissing him lightly on the cheek. He looked as though he had just woken up. His clothes were not ironed, and he was unshaven. Jackson moved forward to get a better look, standing in dog mess in the process.

Are you kidding me? he thought, raising his shoe to inspect the damage. *Jesus*.

She dropped her arms and held her elbow with the opposing hand as they spoke. He looked just as nervous as she did. He moved to one side and Elena entered the house. Jackson got a clear view of the man then, a man he recognised.

WELL, well, well, he thought, *Detective Inspector Graham fucking Walker*.

18

GRAHAM LOOKED UNWELL. Sure, Elena had not seen him for a few weeks, but she never remembered him looking like this. He looked homeless, dishevelled, and not at all like the man she had always called "Dad". That man was powerful, assertive, and exceptionally well presented. The figure standing before her now, with his head low and eyes sunken, was quite the opposite. And she found it distressing.

"You've looked better," she said with a nervous smile.

He said nothing, but turned and motioned through the lounge, towards the kitchen, beyond an open door.

"Come on kid, I'll put the kettle on."

Not much had changed inside the house since she had last been here. It was she who had found the listing for the property online and viewed it with him. They had both said at the time that it would only be for a short while, a stopgap until he found his feet and was in a better position to find something more suitable. Graham had taken the idea literally. What little possessions he had were still packed in cardboard boxes of assorted size and colour that were strewn haphazardly around the house. He had added no furniture, apart from a television and a single, wooden chair in the kitchen. A chair that did not look as though it could support the weight of a grown man, especially not her father.

She stepped over an orange mess on the floor on the way through to the kitchen.

That would explain the smell, she thought, trying to avoid stepping in the coagulated substance before her. *That's been there for a while.*

"I see you've kept Peter alive at least," she said, pointing to the kitchen windowsill.

He chuckled. "Yeah, just about. He's doing better than I am, anyway."

Peter was the only splash of colour in the whole of what Elena could see of the house. A Bonsai Ficus, its trunk twisted magically into an "S" shape, complete with a small rockery in its shallow, porcelain pot. She had bought it for him as a moving in present, and was pleasantly surprised to see it still living, let alone thriving as it was.

Elena walked up to the window and rubbed the waxy leaves between her finger and thumb, being careful not to damage the fragile plant. The kettle was coming to the boil. She turned and opened her mouth to ask him how he was, but he spoke first. He had his back turned to her, preparing the tea, and he caught her off guard.

"I'm going to start rehab, Elena."

He paused for a long moment, his back still turned to her. He was too ashamed, too afraid to face his daughter head on, to see the look of pity and disappointment on her face.

She took him by the hand, turning him on the spot and smiling up at him with an adoring gaze. The same look she had always given him since she was a little girl. A look that said, "I love you". A look that put him immediately at ease.

"That's great news," she replied, beaming up at him. "I'm thrilled for you, and as much as it sucks, it's definitely a step in the right direction."

As far back as she could remember, her father had always drunk. It was only the past few years, when she was in her last years of college and university, that she had fully appreciated the hold it had on him, and the damage it was causing to both him and her mother. As much as she hated to admit it to herself, she believed it had been the catalyst that had driven her parents to divorce, that had driven her mother into the arms of another man.

Graham stirred the cups and squeezed the tea bags on the side. He turned to face his only child, the only light in his life, managing only a weary smile, and motioned to the single chair.

"Take a seat," he said. "How has your mother been?"

"She's okay, I guess." He could tell Elena was hesitant to answer. "Mum calls me, a lot. She thinks I blame her. And she thinks if she bugs me constantly, that it shows she cares."

Elena looked down into her drink. She was nervous, fidgety, as though this was not exactly the conversation she wanted to be having.

"Elena," he said, taking a sip from his mug. "The only thing your mother cares about is that bloody Saturday morning cooking show, and well, the heat from a stranger's cock."

"Dad!" she cried out, laughing hysterically.

Tea shot from her nose and ended up in a puddle on the

kitchen floor. They were both in fits of laughter. She had not heard him laugh for some time, and it made her feel good. It brought back memories, happy, wholesome memories from years past. Memories of her and her dad, running through the park, chasing squirrels together and eating ice cream. Memories of the family on holiday together, soaking up the sun on a beach. Time before the bottled demons took him, before he succumbed to the liquid evil, and it made her feel warm inside.

Wiping tea from her face with her sleeve, she put the cup on the windowsill. "Dad, I have some news."

"Oh god, you're not up the duff, are you?" he replied, still laughing.

She leaned forward and slapped him playfully on the forearm. "No, I'm bloody not. But I have met somebody, actually."

"Oh, Jesus, that's just as bad. Will I have to chase this one off with a cricket bat as well?"

"No. Not this one. This one is special."

"You said that about the last one as well." She hit him on the arm again, which seemed only to fuel his laughter further. "I want to meet him. This Romeo. See if he gets *my* seal of approval."

"To see if he's good enough for your little girl. Please don't make me vom." She motioned as if to put her fingers down her throat. "Anyway, his name is Jackson. He's different to pretty much every other guy I've met."

"And that's a good thing?"

"I think so, yeah."

"Different how?"

She shrugged. "I dunno."

Elena found it impossible to hide her smile as she spoke

about him. Her mind drifted, back to the afternoon under the old tree, something Graham definitely noticed.

"Just different. You'll see, I'll bring him by."

"Like hell you will. I'll tell you what, I'll meet you both somewhere. This place is a bloody tip."

"Yeah, okay. We'll do that. Sounds like a plan."

She took her mug from the sill and drained it. Smiling, she thrust it towards him and jiggled it in mid-air for him to refill it. He complied, grudgingly, and flicked the kettle back on to boil.

"What about you?" she pried.

"What about *me*?" he said, shooting her a sideways glance.

"Anyone on the horizon? What about that beauty who chops people up?"

"She's a forensic pathologist. She doesn't just 'chop people up'. Her name is Ainsley."

"Aye, her. Have you slipped her a cheeky finger on the sly? Behind the bins of the mortuary, maybe?"

Surprise and horror shot across Graham's face as he registered the words that came from his little girl's mouth. She burst into another fit of laughter and tears streamed down her face.

HE SHOOK his head and smirked. "You're the one that needs bloody help. You sound just like your mother."

19

THE VIBRATION RAN through Jackson's training shoe, through his ankle, and up the length of his shin and into his knee, with each rhythmic step. The knee on his left burned a little with each pounding. He winced, but continued running. Further and further, he ran, away from his demons, his past, and towards his fate. He ran on, through the pain.

The first rays of the early morning sun made their way between the clouds and filtered through the patchwork of autumn leaves. They were comforting, and they warmed his body as he picked up the pace.

The sweat was gathering in ever-increasing amounts, forcing the cotton of his tee-shirt to cling unapologetically to his torso. It left nothing to the imagination. His toned physique was there for the world to see, and he wanted to be noticed. Other runners turned and gave him admiring looks as the birds, way up in the trees, sang their sweet morning songs. But he paid no attention. Jackson's attention was elsewhere. His attention was fixed to the sounds filtering into his ears. To the audio from the recent police interviews, playing on repeat. Fuelling him. Powering him forward through his headphones.

Whoever you are, we will find you.

We will find you.

We. Will. Find. You.

The path meandered to the right, then to the left, and underneath a crumbling stone bridge. It passed a small pond, a children's playground and a field with people taking part in an early morning exercise class. The sweat dripped down his face, burning his eyes, but still he ran, still he listened.

We. Will. Find. You.

The feeling underfoot changed. He could feel each stone through the thin sole of his shoe as he crunched onwards through the gravel. He slowed his pace to catch a breath. The brisk morning air flooding his lungs with each forward step.

And there, the tree stood, as it always had, and offered him a sweet respite under its shaded canopy. The view from here was perfect, unobstructed, and the shade let his body cool. He was not here to watch, not this morning. He was not here for morning yoga, a shower, or a pre-breakfast coffee. He was here just to say *hello.* He was slightly too early besides, and he had much to do.

JACKSON COULD FEEL the cold leather of the couch through his shorts. They were still damp from the run, and the lycra clung to him like a second skin. He drained the glass of juice and sat the empty glass down to his left, on top of the dark-stained coffee table. He rubbed his face, deep in thought. He had not shaved for a few days, and he felt scruffy. He had been preoccupied; his thoughts had been elsewhere.

So, who are you then, Mr Walker? he thought, opening the lid of his laptop.

A simple search of his name provided Jackson with a glimpse, an insight into the man at the door.

Elena's father.

Detective Inspector Graham Walker. A celebrated, decorated officer and detective.

He had received attention from the media on several occasions. Although, not always for the right reasons.

"One of South Wales's brightest and best," one article claimed. "Hero detective strikes again," said another.

There was one story, however, that really got Jackson's attention. It dated from several years past, and the man in the photograph was younger then and full of life. Time had not been too kind, it seemed, to Mr. Walker.

"Police chase ends in tragedy," the headline read.

POLICE ARE INVESTIGATING the fatal crash which took place in the Cathays area of Cardiff earlier today.

Thirty-seven-year-old Detective Inspector Michael Dalling and thirty-one-year-old Detective Sergeant Graham Walker were in an unmarked police car giving chase to a suspect, when they were involved in a single vehicle collision.

Despite the best efforts of medical staff and those at the scene, DI Michael Dalling, the passenger, could not be saved.

The driver of the car, DS Graham Walker, was taken to hospital, but his injuries are not believed to be serious.

Detective Inspector Michael Dalling is survived by his wife and two young sons.

South Wales police are now investigating the incident and are encouraging anyone who witnessed it to come forward with information.

JACKSON LEANED back into his seat and cupped his hands around his face. He looked left, out of the window, to the full glory of the morning sun peeking over the horizon. The light filtered in and warmed the space. He could feel it on his arm, his leg, and on his cheek. He closed his eyes, breathed deeply, and exhaled.

Is this why Daddy drinks? he thought to himself, scanning the article again. *Is this the moment that your family crumbled?*

Know your enemies, he thought, peering down at his phone.

Elena had only messaged yesterday, asking him to meet her and Graham in a café in town for a coffee, and he was happy to oblige, happy to meet the man in person. To get a sense of *him* face to face. To see if he knew. Jackson had a keen instinct for reading people, and perhaps Graham did as well.

Know your enemies and keep them close.

He was not scared of getting caught. In truth, it had never even crossed his mind. He thought, no, he believed he was better than *them*. Smarter than *them*. One step ahead. Elena's father was just another small obstacle. One that he must overcome, whatever the cost. It excited him, aroused him even, and brought his skin to shivering gooseflesh.

He stared at the photo of the man on his computer with a wide smile. His eyes were alive with fire, and he could feel the adrenalin coursing through his veins. He picked up the laptop with his clammy hands, holding it at arm's length. He laughed hysterically, spinning around, as if he were dancing with Graham himself.

Let's play, shall we, Mr Walker.

Faster and faster he spun, laughing at the screen. The laugh of a man possessed. The laugh of a man obsessed. Spinning, spinning, spinning in a fit of near maniacal hysteria.

Let's play. Let's play. Let's play.

THE DRIVE to work was pleasant, considering the traffic. Jackson pulled into a space and shifted the car into 'park'. He could still smell the piney notes from the air freshener hanging from the mirror. He had not taken the car to be washed for some time, but inside it was still gleaming, as he liked it.

He spied Joel across the car park and gave him a friendly wave. The man had been elated since the night of the launch. He had also met a girl, and if his social media feeds were anything to go by, things seemed to be going well.

Keeps him off my back for now, I suppose.

Jackson could not afford to be distracted. Not now. He had to plan. He had to be on his game. He had to be focused.

Jackson peered down at the lock screen of his phone and smiled with pride. He kissed the end of his finger and pressed it gently to the screen. To *her* lips.

SOON IT WILL JUST BE *us, my love.*

20

POLICE CONSTABLE LEWIS REED struggled to catch his breath. His lungs gasped for air in the harsh winter cold, and the muscles in his calves and thighs ached and burned. Sweat travelled down the length of his face and leached into his mouth, leaving a lingering, salty taste. It tasted like success, and the burning in his legs, however unpleasant, was well earned. The man underneath him, handcuffed, face down on the concrete, was a testament to that.

He had chased the man, a petty thief who had swiped a woman's purse as she stood in line for an ATM, for close on a mile. They had managed to traverse a good amount of the city centre in their time together. Through the town itself, slaloming between shoppers and young families, coming close to knocking one poor old lady down flat on her face, and then down winding dark alleys. Lewis could feel the discomforting crunch of discarded needles underfoot, and the glazed over, almost dead-looking eyes of the people that had used them, following him.

They emerged at the edge of a park, one of the city's numerous dog-shit minefields, and ran clear through a children's game of football. Their presence did little to interrupt play, and the game continued around them as if they were nothing more than a pair of passing phantoms. Lewis closed the gap across the grass. Maybe the thief was tiring, or perhaps Lewis had better traction in his police issued boots, but either way he was only an arm's length behind.

As they reached the edge of the playing field, the thief came a cropper on a stray kerb and went crashing to the concrete with an audible thud, the contents of the lady's purse spilling into the street. Lewis was on him immediately, knee pressed into his back. The man on the ground voiced his discontent aloud to whoever would listen. A few people stopped to gawk, some took out their phones to snap photographs, others shuffled away, guarding their children's eyes and ears. Lewis pushed his face into the dirt with a satisfying crunch to silence him, and read him his rights.

HE ONLY HAD a few days left in uniform. From Monday, Lewis' transfer to CID would be official, and this had been a most gratifying way to see out his time as a PC. He would work alongside DI Walker, a man he had admired since the beginning of his brief career. A man who, for a time, was like a celebrity around the station, and it was not only Lewis who looked up to him. Men wanted to be just like him, women just wanted to be *under* him.

The higher you climb, the harder you fall, Lewis' dad had once told him, and Graham Walker was a prime example. Lewis saw through the clouds of speculation and accusations to a fine man and police officer who only needed a second chance, someone to help him, to guide him back to glory, and Lewis felt *he* was that man.

If he was honest to himself, Lewis was nothing if not magnanimous. He saw the good where there was only bad, light where there were only shadows. He wanted nothing more than to help and fix, to put back the pieces, and bring the dead back to life. He saw a project in Graham. He wanted to be the blacksmith who would take him into the fire and re-forge his life. He never expected, however, during the process, to find a friend amongst the rubble.

SEPTEMBER 21ST 2018, 18:50

THEIR SHIFT HAD FINISHED NEARLY an hour ago, and the sun had almost set, but Lewis and Graham sat on the low wall around the station car park, chatting. Graham flicked the dead end of his cigarette to the ground and lifted the collar of his jacket to protect his neck from the early evening chill. The sky was clear, and the beginnings of stars were just visible through the haze of the city lights.

"I have my first meeting later on tonight, Lew."

"Shitting it?"

"Oh, completely mate. Sitting around, talking about feelings and hugging fucking strangers. Sounds like a right laugh."

He took a fresh cigarette from its packet and lit it, exhaling a cloud of blue smoke into the chilly, evening breeze.

"You need this. Jesus, Gray, *I* need this." Both men laughed aloud. "How's Elena doing?"

Of all the people he had worked with over the years, the various partners and colleagues, it had only ever been Lewis Reed who had brought light into his face, and warmth into his heart. And if truth be told, he loved him for it.

"Yeah, she's doing alright, better than I am anyway. She's got a new boyfriend, so she was smiling ear to ear when I saw her last."

The vibration coming from Graham's jacket pocket abruptly interrupted the pair's conversation. He pinched his cigarette between his lips and answered his phone.

"Walker."

"Got some news for you, sir," the voice on the other end of the line started. "Been digging through CCTV from around the area where Jessica Evans was discovered and got a partial plate from a car that matches your description. It was spotted in the area around about the right time. Once on a village shop's camera and again on a post office one, a few minutes apart."

"Go on," he replied. He pointed to Lewis, and then to his phone, as if to signal the importance of the call.

"Black, '99 Volvo Estate. First three characters of the registration are V32. Crappy old grainy cameras, but it's a start."

"Was the number plate obstructed?"

"Hard to tell, but it could have been by the look of it, yeah. I'll call back if we get anything else."

"Thanks mate."

Graham ended the call and turned to Lewis, lighting yet another cigarette, this one off the end of the other, and smiled.

"We got our car."

"Whose is it?" Lewis asked, almost jumping to his feet.

"Not a bloody clue, clever prick disguised the plate, but

they can't hide forever. We'll find it." He pulled back the sleeve of his mock-tweed jacket and gazed blankly at his wristwatch. "Shit, mate, I have to shoot."

Graham stood and patted his partner on the back and shot him a heartfelt smile. As he turned and made his way towards his car, he put his hand in the air and shouted back to Lewis.

"Wish me luck, boyo."

JACKSON COULD SEE his breath in the freezing night air. It drifted on the breeze, dissipating under the dim glow of the streetlights. The trees around him swayed, and high up in the canopy, something rustled. A bird? Or a squirrel perhaps. There would be a frost tonight, he knew, he could feel it in his bones, and on the soft skin of his face and hands. He was crouched low, creeping in the underbrush, stalking his prey from the shadows. He could see her here, as clear as day from his lonely, covered perch.

Jackson held his breath in admiration as she transitioned from pyramid to warrior-two. The toned muscles of her stomach flexed as her body moved with majesty through the positions. Blood rushed to his trousers, and he stood alone in the cold, aroused.

His breathing deepened and sweat gathered underneath his clothes.

My Elena, he thought to himself. *Mine.* His eyes were fixated on her window. His mind was there, and only there.

He heard voices approaching. He looked to his right and saw a couple, hand in hand, strolling in his direction. They looked as though they were returning from a date, a nice meal for two, or perhaps a romantic film.

They passed in front of him, a little too close for comfort, and he had to move back into the branches of the tree to avoid being seen. He lowered his breathing as they passed, and he caught the scent of the girl's perfume on the chilly breeze.

Not you, he thought. Not my type.

By the time they had walked far enough down the street, Elena's window was dark, and he could see no more.

No MATTER, *he thought* and pulled a cold grimace. *There's always tomorrow.*

21

September 22nd 2018, 16:45

Graham had to drain the bathtub with a spoon. He had to reach in up to his elbows in water and suds and fish it out. The click-clack mechanism for the plug had stopped working a day or two after he had moved in, and the shower, much to his annoyance, never had. He had thought to bring it up with his landlord, but that jumped up little prick was a pain to deal with at the best of times. He couldn't imagine he'd have been overly enthusiastic to jump at the chance to send a plumber out to resolve the issues, at his own cost.

The meeting the night before had gone about as well as he could have hoped. There was crying, a lot of it, and some forced hugging that was part of some trust exercise. But Graham had mostly stayed quiet and listened.

"Hi, I'm Graham, and I am an alcoholic," had been the extent of his interactions.

Listening to strangers drone on about their problems for an hour and a half had made him want to dive, headfirst, out of the first story window and run to the closet pub. But he was not there for him, as much as he was there for Elena, and, well, to keep his job and sanity.

The evening's antics behind him, Graham stood outside next to his Jeep, smoking a cigarette, exhaling blue smoke into the evening breeze with a sigh of relief.

Maybe this could be good, he thought. *Maybe it will work if I want it to.*

Through a confidence whose origin he could not place, he took out his phone and dialled Ainsley's number.

"I would love to, Gray," she had said when he asked her to meet up for a quiet dinner and chat. "Your place sounds great."

HE HAD THOUGHT TO COOK, but Elena, in her infinite wisdom, had talked him out of it.

"How about we concentrate on making you, and this shit hole, look half presentable," she had said when she'd called round earlier that afternoon. "Besides, your cooking sucks, and you don't want to make her sick on your first date. Be safe, order out."

She had helped him clean the house, iron some clothes and ordered him to shave. She even had a fun activity planned for them before his date: the assembly of a Swedish flat pack table and chairs so that they wouldn't have to eat on the floor or over the sink. Before she left, Elena set the table, lit a few candles, and placed Peter on the table as a centre piece.

"It looks great, kid, thanks."

"Don't mention it," she replied and kissed him lightly on the cheek. "Just try to have fun, and don't do anything *I* wouldn't. Don't be silly, wrap your—"

"I got it." He laughed. "Now bugger off before she gets here."

Ainsley was on time, although that didn't surprise him, and she looked magnificent. She had been knocked back a few times by bad relationships, and he imagined it took a whole heap of energy to work as she did. But none of that seemed to stop her. She oozed a cool, sexual confidence that was clear by her choice of outfit and the way she held herself.

"I've brought wine for me, and some non-alcoholic monstrosity that they try to sell as wine, for you," she said, grinning as she stood in the doorway.

"Funny," he replied, returning the smile. "Come in, please."

Like a gentleman, he took her coat and put the bottles to chill in the fridge. She radiated a warmth into the house that had been missing in Graham's life for some time. It felt alien, but at the same time, it felt completely like home.

"You look fab, Ainz." His voice was shaky.

She smiled and looked at him through her hazel eyes with adoring admiration. "You're not looking too shabby yourself, Mr. Walker."

They crossed the threshold into the living room, and Ainsley beamed at the table laid out before her. She took him by the hand and kissed him gently on the cheek.

"Now, I know full well this was not your doing."

"Guilty," he replied. He blushed when she kissed him, his heart fluttered, and he began to sweat lightly. "The kid didn't trust me not to mess this up."

She giggled innocently behind her hand, like a school-girl hearing a rude joke or word for the first time, as she made her way further into the room. Graham pulled out a chair for her at the table. The single candle cast a shadow over the soft lines of her face. He had forgotten how uniquely beautiful she truly was. He had forgotten what it was like to want another.

"I'll get us a couple of drinks," he said, walking towards the kitchen. "Chinese or Indian?"

"Indian all the way," she replied. "I could do with a little spice in my life."

Graham turned back, and she gazed at him seductively from underneath her lashes. In the dim candlelight she looked half her age, and he felt half of his as their eyes met. They were like two school friends, parents out of the house, alone for the first time.

GRAHAM DRAINED the glass of water in front of him as he pushed the plate to one side. Beads of sweat had gathered on his forehead, and he was visibly flushed.

"You're such a baby," Ainsley jested as she put her cutlery down and picked up her wineglass.

"I made an error in judgement, that curry is too bloody hot," he replied, coughing.

This put her into a fit of laughter. She held her hand to her face not to spit wine all over the table.

"Men and their bravado. Just order a korma next time and bloody enjoy it."

He lifted his head and dotted his brow with a napkin. Damp patches had appeared through his shirt.

"Next time?" he asked sheepishly.

"Well, I should hope so. My company is not that bad I hope."

"Definitely not."

He took her hand in his and rubbed it affectionately

with his thumb. This was the most comfortable, the most whole he had felt for a long time. Her face seemed to mirror the same feeling, and that only reinforced his fondness for her.

"So, who is this new guy Elena is seeing?" she asked, gathering the empty food cartons together.

"I don't know a lot about him. I'm meeting them for coffee tomorrow in town. She's keen I meet him."

"Any idea what he looks like?"

"None. All I know is that he's a designer, or an illustrator or something, works in the city."

Ainsley took the phone from her bag and swiped it open, clicking the icon of a social media application.

"What's his name?"

"Jackson Page, I think she said."

She looked at her screen for a long moment, puzzled. She swiped her finger up and down the screen, but said nothing. Finally, she lifted her head.

"It seems lover boy is a bit of a ghost."

"How do you mean?"

"He doesn't exist. Well, not on here anyway. Strange for a lad of his age. Gray, are you okay?"

His face was frozen in a mix of confusion and mild terror. His breathing was slow and deep, purposeful. His eyes seemed to have almost glazed over. He looked like he had just seen a ghost.

"I'm fine," he finally replied. "I'm sure it's nothing."

"It doesn't look like nothing," she replied, screwing her face up.

He lifted his head and forced a smile. "It's nothing, honestly. Would you like some more wine?"

Hesitantly, she answered. "Sure, why not. Graham, if there's something up you can tell me."

"I know, and I will. Honestly, it's nothing."

He returned from the kitchen, fresh bottle in hand, and sat back at the table, giving her a wide, heartfelt smile. After filling her glass, he took her hand and kissed it gently.

"Will you stay with me tonight, Ainz?"

HE LAY there in the dark, eyes skyward towards the blank ceiling. Ainsley was breathing gently next to him. She was sound asleep, her arm interlocked with his. But he could not drift off. He could smell the sweet scent of coconut on her hair and her presence made him feel good. It calmed him, made him feel whole. But something was nagging, clawing at the back of his mind. And he could not seem to let it lie.

WHY IS HE HIDING? he thought. *What is he hiding?*

22

She smiled at him, across the counter, and Jackson felt that familiar itch.

"Oat latte for Jackson," she called out, knowing full well whose it was. She had not taken her eyes from him since he had arrived.

"Thanks Becky," he said coolly, taking the cup from her hand and reading the name badge pinned to her breast.

He brushed his finger against hers and they locked eyes. She blushed, and he could see her breathing change.

"You're welcome," she said with a flirtatious grin. "Any time."

Jackson took a seat in a booth with seating for four. The table had not been thoroughly cleaned, although he swore he could smell a lemony scent. But there were crumbs strewn across it, and his sleeve stuck to the top as he sat his cup down.

How hard is it? he thought.

He was sitting facing the counter, towards the barista with pert breasts, who was gazing in his direction periodically and not hiding the fact well. He enjoyed that, perhaps a little too much. The longer he sat and watched, the more she stared, and the less she tried to hide it.

ON CUE, at ten past the hour, Elena entered the café with Detective Inspector Walker. She looked as ever, incredible, dressed in her chequered shirt and dungaree combination, complete with heavy, dark boots. Her father wore a crisp blue shirt and black jeans. It even looked as though he had recently shaved. They made their way over to the table, Elena smiling as she strode. Graham seemed less enthused, perhaps even visibly anxious. Jackson stood to great them and extended a hand.

"Mr. Robinson, it's a pleasure," he said, shaking Graham's hand enthusiastically.

"It's Walker. Robinson is Elena's mother's name, and less of the mister. Just call me Graham."

Jackson smiled in acceptance, knowing full well the situation at hand. He was merely prodding the beast, testing the water to see if it would bare its teeth.

He turned and embraced Elena, kissing her gently. "Hey you."

"Hey yourself," she replied.

Jackson slid down the booth, and she took a seat next to him.

"Shall I get us some fresh drinks?" Jackson asked.

"It's okay, I got it," Graham replied. "You two catch up. Oat milk is it, kid?"

"Please. That would be great, thanks."

Graham headed to the counter, not once looking back at

the pair. Jackson did not like the feeling he was already getting from the man. He was cold, distant, calculating.

Can you smell me, Mr. Walker? he thought.

"He seems nice," Jackson said, draining the last of his coffee.

"He's not normally so quiet, I think he's shitting himself a little, so be nice."

She punched the top of his arm playfully, biting her bottom lip seductively as she smiled.

"I'll try my best," he replied.

GRAHAM RETURNED to the table with the drinks and a blueberry muffin for Elena. He put on his best fake smile and sat opposite the pair. He took his phone from the top pocket of his jacket and put it on silent mode, placing it down, broken screen first, on the table. Graham studied the man in front of him for a long moment, and as he did, Jackson locked eyes with him, sliding his hand across the table and gripping Elena's.

Graham considered his words carefully. Perhaps a little too carefully, as the pause felt borderline rude. He did not have a good feeling about the man sitting before him, smiling with an overt confidence and holding his daughter's hand, brandishing her as if she were his own, a prize he had won, or was winning. The look Jackson gave him, an unmoving and unblinking stare, got his hackles up. And the hairs on his neck stood on end as a chill travelled the length of his spine.

What's with you? Graham thought.

There was something about him, something that Graham could not yet put his finger on, but it made him feel as though he were in competition with him, as if he had been unknowingly entered into a contest, with Elena being the prize.

Graham put the warm mug to his lips and drank deeply, wiping his mouth with the rough back of his hand as he put the cup back down to rest.

"So, how did you kids meet?" he asked.

"At a book launch," Jackson replied as he rubbed Elena's hand. She was beaming back at him, seemingly unaware of the brewing tension. "We just bumped into each other at the buffet table and got talking."

"Cute," Graham replied, taking another long sip of coffee.

Try as he might, he could not seem to lose Jackson's gaze. His eyes seemed to follow him everywhere. It was like he was transfixed – hypnotised – like a snake coiling to strike at its prey. It was doing nothing to quell Graham's fast brewing distrust of him, and although she seemed happy, something inside him was vaguely afraid for his daughter.

What the fuck is up with you, kid?

"So, I hear you're a bit of a ghost, Jackson Page," Graham said from behind his raised mug.

"Dad?"

"You've been doing some research?" Jackson replied smugly.

"A friend of mine was curious to have a look, to see who Elena was getting herself involved with."

"And you were not?" Jackson leaned forward, grinning.

Graham lowered his mug and smiled. "I won't lie to you. I was, am, intrigued."

ELENA SHOT LOOKS between the two men, not exactly sure what was unfolding before her as an ambulance, with its sirens wailing, hurtled down the road outside and broke Jackson's gaze. He peered over Graham's shoulder and was pleasantly surprised to see the young barista still looking over. She was fussing with her apron and, if he was not mistaken, she had loosened a button or two from her tight, black shirt.

Too easy, he thought.

"Elena tells me you're a police officer."

"I am. A detective, actually."

"That's pretty cool."

"Yes, it is," Elena said. "He and his partner Lewis have solved some pretty gnarly stuff recently."

Jackson smirked. "Partner?"

"Work partner," Graham replied flatly.

"He's dad's best mate as well. You'd like him. It's his birthday soon, isn't it, Dad?"

Graham nodded silently, not sparing her a glance.

"Have you two had anything to do with that grisly murder everyone's talking about? The one with the mask."

Graham seemed to lose a breath. "We haven't made a lot of headway with that one yet, unfortunately."

"Such a shame," Jackson said.

His tone was sincere, but his eyes, his eyes were cold, dead almost. And Graham could swear he saw the beginning of a grin appear at the corner of the young man's mouth. He rapped the ends of his fingers on the tabletop, buying himself the few precious seconds he needed to construct his next sentence carefully.

"May I ask how you know about the mask? We've been pretty tight-lipped about any details so far. Especially one as sensitive as that."

The young man scoffed, giving Graham a toothy grin. "I suppose I must have just heard it somewhere. You know what it's like. Juicy details like that don't stay secret for too long in today's society."

JACKSON ROLLED the sleeve of his plaid shirt and peered down at his wristwatch. "Oh, look at that. I'm sorry," he said, "but I have to dash."

Elena stood, and he slid gracefully from the booth, stood, embraced her, and kissed her passionately on the lips. "I'll call you later."

"Can't wait," she replied, smiling up at him.

He again extended his hand to Graham. "Great to meet you, sir. We should do this again. How about dinner next Friday? My treat."

"How could I say no?" Graham said.

Jackson gave Graham a sly wink as he released his hand.

"I'll see you tomorrow, beautiful, still on for six?"

"Absolutely," she replied, kissing him.

GRAHAM RECOILED in his seat as Jackson released his grip. He said nothing, but stared blankly, and offered only a slight grin as the young man left. He did not speak even when Elena told him she was going to use the loo.

Did that just happen? he thought.

He leaned forward, rubbing his face with both hands. The stubble was returning in full force, and he would have to shave again if he hoped to see Ainsley again soon. But that wink. That cold, sly flicker and gleam.

Was that just for me? Did Elena see it as well?

His stomach told him one thing, the look on his daughter's face today, and when she had spoken of him before, another. But he could not shake the feeling that something was more than a bit off.

You're just being paranoid, old man, he told himself as he stared from out of the booth and into the void.

"Dad, are you ready? Hello? Earth to Graham."

He came back to reality with a snap. "Sorry kid, I was miles away."

"Everything okay?"

"Absolutely. Come on you, let's go."

"Ainsley worked you hard last night, aye?" she said, laughing hard as she slipped into her jacket.

"YEAH," he replied. "Something like that."

23

THE BOY with the blue backpack stood alone in the middle of the corridor. The floor squeaked underfoot as people passed, the sound of their footsteps resonating off the worn, stained linoleum. He was alone there, in that institute of many. Only one person paid him any attention, a woman much older than he, and she had her own twisted, perverse version of friendship.

The days were long there and the nights cold. The other boys in his room had tried, in vain, to steal his things and hurt him. He did what his father would have done, if he were still alive, as much as it got him into trouble. Jackson figured early on that nobody was coming for him, to offer him the warmth and comfort of a family home. He was too far gone, too broken to love.

Solitude was passed with reading and drawing, with imagining a life beyond those walls. Imagining a life that could have been, a life that would be.

.   .   .

SHE CALLED TO HIM, his friend, and motioned to him with a single finger to follow her into *that* room. She closed the door with a *click*, and turned the key.

24

GRAHAM AWOKE THAT MORNING, finding himself somewhat clear-headed and refreshed. He could hear Ainsley finishing up in the shower that Elena had somehow managed to fix on her last visit, and he knew he would get to kiss her again when she came down. And once again as she made her way out of his front door later that morning.

He was enjoying his newly acquired sobriety. Although he realised that he was one hell of a long way off being well again, the lack of any sort of hangover or regret from the night before was definitely refreshing. However, that left him with more mental capacity and time to think, and that again would have been another positive. But when there was not one, but two, unsolved murders hanging over you, that space to think itself becomes nothing more than a burden. Especially when your overbearing DCI was on the phone at all hours, hoping you would have fabricated a thread of evidence from nothing more than hopes, dreams, and good manners. Not that he showed it, but Graham was seeing a pattern develop, almost a case of déjà vu. Body dumped. Big media fuss. Lack of evidence. Rinse, wash and repeat. And he had to stop it. Somehow.

Luckily, if said person had a time-consuming and menial task to complete, one that they had been putting off for months, then the ability to mull over facts while undistracted becomes somewhat easier. Graham had such a task. And it stared him in the face each morning as he descended the stairs and made for the kitchen.

All the boxes from the move, bar a few that contained essentials like underwear and tea bags, had yet to be unpacked. That was job number one for the day. Job number two was the construction of the flat pack furniture due for delivery later that morning. It was time for him to make that house a home.

Ainsley kissed him passionately on her way out. She was in the shower longer than expected, and as a result she was in a rush. So he improvised and made her a romantic breakfast to go.

"Eggs, soft one side, stringy bits taken off the bacon, coffee, one sugar."

"Christ, you are more than a pretty face, detective."

"I try my best. Have a good one. Ring me when you finish."

"You too, speak to you later." She kissed him once more, and she was gone.

That one may be a keeper, he thought to himself, smiling.

HE TURNED to look at the stack of boxes piled to his left and groaned.

"I guess it's just us then guys," he said.

After the first few boxes, Graham quickly realised why Olivia had not put up much of a fight when he was packing up things to move out. He had left in a hurry, chucking whatever he could into cardboard boxes, in a whirlwind of blind emotion, so much so that he had not stopped to consider what most of it even was. That was, besides his clothes.

Half of this is useless tat, he thought. *Shite we collected over the years and just never got round to throwing away. No wonder she was glad to be rid of it.*

Most of what came out of the boxes was not-so-gently put back in. He sealed them up with brown packing tape as he went and scribbled the word "tip" on the front with a heavy black marker. The "tip" boxes were then piled by the front door.

There was a knock at the door just after noon. Although pissed at the tardiness, Graham smiled and showed the delivery men where to put the furniture. He thanked them for their help, and even tipped them generously as they left. By this point, there was only a single box left to unpack.

A small box, perhaps half a foot cubed in size, and neatly taped up, sat at the base of the stairs. Its compact size and neat presentation made him feel oddly uneasy. He had no recollection of packing it. He picked it up. It was incredibly light, regardless of its small size. He shook it, and could hear only a faint rustling coming from within. He took it into the living room, put it on the table, and opened it. He most definitely did not pack *this* box.

The box contained several envelopes. Each sealed with a kiss in red lipstick, his name written on the front in a neat hand. Each containing a letter. Graham's heart stopped for a moment and then jumped into his throat. He could swear he could smell his ex-wife's perfume wafting gently toward his nose as he picked up each envelope and inspected it. He swallowed hard, took a seat at the table, and opened the first letter.

Graham,

I know, I understand how busy you are, but babe, we need you. Come back to us. I have started writing you these letters because I cannot speak to you, cannot confront you face to face. It's like you look straight through me, and through Elena, too.

I am writing these in the hope that one day you will read them, when everything is back to normal, when we are us again, that they will keep you there where you belong.

Come back to us.

Yours, always.

O x.

His eyes filled, and he closed them. He slowed his breathing, and upon reopening his eyes, he could see that his hands were shaking. He stared blankly at the letter for a long moment, folded it neatly, and returned it carefully to its envelope. Then he took the next letter, slid his finger carefully under the flap, and opened it.

Graham,

I'm taking Elena to my mother's. I do not know how long we will be gone for, if you even notice at all. There is dinner in the fridge.

I don't know how much longer I can do this. I miss you. I miss us.

Come back to me.

O x.

AGAIN, he returned the letter to its envelope. He stood and made his way into the kitchen, where he stared vacantly out of the window and into the garden, waiting for the kettle to boil. He noticed for the first time that the garden that he once took for a dumping ground had some real potential. It was overgrown, yes, and full of rubbish, but it was a good size and south facing.

With a bit of work, it could be okay. Somewhere to sit and relax when summer finally rolls by, he thought.

Graham returned to the table, cup in hand and sat. He rummaged to the bottom of the box and took out the final letter in the pile. He put the envelope to his face, closed his eyes and inhaled. The sweet, unmistakable scent of his first true love filled his airways. In his mind he was transported back to years gone by and it brought an unwelcome lump to his throat. He exhaled slowly, and opened it.

GRAHAM,

This, I am afraid, will be my final letter to you. God knows I have tried to help, fucking hell, to fix you. But you are too far gone for even me to find.

I will always love the man I knew, the man who I fell for in the mountains, the man who asked me to marry him down by the river. But I do not love you anymore. In my heart I do not even know who you are.

Don't hate me, but I have met someone else.

O x.

.   .   .

GRAHAM RETURNED the letter to its envelope, and that in turn, to the box. He swallowed hard, managing to expel his heart from his throat, re-sealed the box, and piled it at the door with the others destined for the rubbish tip.

He took a moment, closed his eyes, and breathed deeply. Much to his surprise, his hands were no longer shaking when he re-opened them. They had been shaking a lot recently, perhaps unsurprisingly, but they were still now. He lifted them to his face, palms facing, and after inspecting them in amazement, rubbed his face rigorously and began to laugh.

I AM NO LONGER that man, Liv, the man by the river is coming back, and this time he is here to stay.

25

Much to Lewis' surprise, and somewhat to his own, Graham arrived at the office on time the following morning. And he looked well. He took a seat at his desk with an uncharacteristic smile on his face and, perhaps more surprisingly, a coffee for both him and Lewis. DCI Morgan had called a briefing, a weekly update of sorts, to establish their position on the double murders, and whether they were, in fact, making any headway in the case. Graham had got to the station early to make sure he had time for a stiff caffeine fix before it all kicked off, and to catch up with Lewis.

"Who are you and what the bloody hell have you done with my mate?"

Graham chuckled, handing the steaming mug over the top of a computer monitor.

"Hilarious. I am allowed to smile once in a while."

"Yeah, I agree, but this is just fucking creepy. I'm

expecting tentacles to sprout from your ears, or for you to pull off an extremely convincing Graham mask and have some horrid lizard face underneath. Honestly, though, is everything okay?"

Graham stared at him blankly and then smirked. "Everything is great. For the first time in a long while, I can honestly say that to you without lying through my teeth."

Graham had done a lot of thinking the previous afternoon. The letters had brought home some cold hard truths but had also led him to the realisation of the man he wanted to be, the man he needed to be. They had highlighted and brought into focus what and who was important, what really mattered.

In the case of his daughter, it was her new boyfriend that was making her happy. Graham thought he was being too hasty, that perhaps the lad was a bit different, and that he should give him the benefit of the doubt, if only for her. His instincts had proved to serve him well in the past, but maybe this time they had been clouded by the powerful urge to protect her, that because he had not always been there for her, that he needed now more than ever to keep her safe. She seemed to like him after all; she seemed to trust him, and perhaps he could as well, in time.

He was meeting them after work for dinner. He was bringing Ainsley along too, a sort of father-daughter double date. He would be nice to Jackson tonight, strike up conversation, or at least he would try. He could not risk upsetting Elena, not again.

DCI Morgan appeared in front of the whiteboard, removed his jacket, and took a long draw on the disposable coffee cup in his hand.

"Ladies and gentlemen, if you're ready," he said, throwing the cup into a nearby wastepaper basket.

The team gathered around Morgan. There was a look of determination crossed with exhaustion on the faces of everyone present. This was proving to be a tough case to crack, with little to nothing to show for the combined effort of all the people in that room.

"I would like to start by saying a massive thank you to you all. For the effort everyone is, and I imagine will continue to expend on bringing the people or person responsible for the deaths of these young women, and the pain and continued suffering of their families, to justice. I wish I could be stood here sharing some game-changing piece of information. But sadly, that is not the case. We will continue to focus on two main lines of enquiry: the car, and the possibility of any connection that may have existed between the victims." Morgan surveyed the faces in front of him. Everyone remained silent, focused. "Andrews, where are we with the Volvo?"

"Nowhere as of yet, sir. We're looking into any other possible sightings of the vehicle with the V registration and are still in the process of attempting to cross reference a car with that description with known offenders."

"Good, okay. And Graham, Lewis, anything of use for us yet?"

"We have a theory," Graham replied.

"We're all ears, Mr. Walker. Please, go on."

"We think we are looking at one killer. A young man, probably. Late twenties, early thirties, charming, good-looking, judging by the looks of the two victims." He paused for a second, realising the similarities to who he was describing, and quickly shook it off.

"And how the bloody hell would you know that?" Morgan asked.

"We have acquired some archival phone records for both of our victims from their respective service providers." Graham motioned to the file on his lap. "Now, unfortunately, they show no indication of any communication with anyone that could be considered a boyfriend in the weeks and days leading up to their deaths. But that does not mean that they hadn't met someone."

"What are you getting at?"

"It was something that Harriet, Jessica's housemate, said. She said Jessica was due to see a guy, to go on a date with him. So she must have met him somehow. And the lack of correspondence to anyone like that bothers me."

"Right, okay, but as far as anyone knew at the time, Sophie was not seeing anyone," Morgan said.

"I know, I thought the same thing, but what if we were asking the wrong questions?"

The room fell silent, and Graham let his words hang in the air for a moment before continuing.

"We had no reason to suspect a possible boyfriend at the time, and her parents almost laughed the idea off. Look, it's just a feeling, I know that. But someone picked Jessica up in large, black car. This person, this mystery Romeo, and the driver of the Volvo, could be the same guy."

Everyone in the room exchanged looks of fascination. Andrews, sitting at the back, looked a tad uncomfortable at the thought, however.

Graham continued, "We were looking through some of the notes, from the conversations we had with people after Sophie was found, and if anyone knew about a guy she was seeing, it will be her."

He held up a photograph of a young woman with shoulder-length blonde hair and striking blue eyes.

Stern intrigue crossed DCI Morgan's face. He put his hand to his cheek, and paused for a long moment.

"Who is she?" Morgan asked finally, letting out a long sigh.

"Her name is Isabelle Turner. She was Sophie's supposed best friend. We spoke to her on a number of occasions, but she became hysterical each time and we didn't manage to extract anything of use from her."

"You think she might know something?"

"No idea. But if she saw a car, saw a guy, maybe, then at least we know we're looking in the right direction. It at least would give us a solid connection between Jessica and Sophie."

"Fine, okay, bring her in."

"She's on her way, sir. Detective Reed spoke to her on the phone briefly yesterday. She was at work so couldn't talk for long, but agreed to come down for a chat later on this morning."

"Okay, brilliant, let me know if you get anything from her."

Graham nodded. "Sir."

Morgan turned and motioned to the photographs of the two girls taped to the board behind him. He spoke faster, his voice slightly raised, his eyes wide and fierce.

"We cannot lose morale, guys. There is something here, or someone out there, that will connect the dots, and we *will* find it. Let's keep it going, thanks."

He waved them off and retreated into the corridor where his office was located. Graham slapped Lewis on the leg as he pulled himself up out of his chair with a groan, and gave his young partner a wink.

"You heard the man, kid. Hop to."

ISABELLE TURNER WAS ALREADY WAITING in the reception area by the time Graham and Lewis got downstairs. A pretty young woman of perhaps twenty-one. She was extremely well dressed and stood just to the left of the main doors, oozing a calm, sexual confidence that was borderline stand-offish. But there was something behind her eyes, Graham noticed upon greeting her, pain, or an untold sadness perhaps.

"Miss Turner? Detective Inspector Graham Walker, thank you for coming in at such short notice. This is my colleague Detective Sergeant Lewis Reed, who you spoke on the phone with yesterday."

"Nice to meet you both," she replied from behind a feigned smile, almost a grimace. "No problem at all."

"Would you like to go somewhere quieter to talk?" Graham said, motioning to the few people sat in the reception area.

One man, with a freshly shaved head and dirtied trousers, was holding a tissue to his nose to stem some bleeding. He looked as though he should have been in a hospital waiting area, not one at a police station.

"Yeah, that would be great, thanks."

"Can I get you a tea or coffee, perhaps?"

"Tea would be great, thanks. White, no sugar."

GRAHAM FOUND AN UNUSED INTERVIEW ROOM, through a set of heavy double doors and down a corridor that came off the main reception area. He turned on the light as they entered and pulled out a seat for their guest.

"As DC Reed said on the phone yesterday, we are following up on some of our previous enquiries in relation to the disappearance and subsequent death of your friend Sophie. We believe that whoever was responsible is still at large, and could also be responsible for another, more recent murder."

"That Jessica girl from Cathays?" Isabelle replied, somewhat colder than Graham was expecting.

"Yes, that's correct."

"Like I said on the phone, Detective Walker—"

"Please, call me Graham."

"Like I said on the phone, Detective *Graham*, I don't think there is a lot more I could tell you."

He didn't like her tone. She seemed almost defensive, and by the look on Lewis' face, the feeling was mutual.

"Did Sophie have a boyfriend? Was she seeing anyone?"

Isabelle took a long sip from her plastic disposable cup before answering. "I wouldn't know."

"It says here," Lewis said, flicking through a file, "that you were living together at the time of Miss Jones' disappearance, and that you considered yourself to be her *best* friend."

Clutching the cup firmly between her hands, Isabelle looked down at the table in front of her, her eyes seeming to dart from left to right. Her voice became a little shaky.

"No, that's not right, we lived together, sure, but we were not that close."

Graham leaned in close, almost close enough to smell her. He rested his elbow on the table and cupped his freshly shaven face in one hand.

"So, how *would* you describe your relationship to the deceased?"

Isabelle was silent for a long moment. And in that time,

the time she used to consider her words, she avoided all eye contact with the pair, and she tapped the ends of her fingers lightly on the tabletop.

"Complicated," she eventually choked out in what was almost a whisper.

"How so?"

"We... I mean, she was a bit of a free spirit, you know. And things could be a little one sided sometimes."

"From your end?"

"Yeah."

She still refused to look up at Graham as he spoke.

"Isabelle, is there... sorry, *was* there, more to your relationship. Did you have feelings for her?"

Caught off guard, she recoiled into her chair. She paused, mouth agape, staring at the cup in front of her in silence.

"I'm sorry?" she eventually said, sounding almost as if she were wounded.

"Sophie, did you have romantic feelings for her?"

"I... I mean no, I couldn't have... not me..."

"Not you, because of your father?"

She threw a look at Graham that suggested that he had struck a nerve, or perhaps re-opened a healing wound. Her top lip trembled, and her blue eyes, striking as they were, glazed over and filled up. Graham slid the file from in front of Lewis to himself and flicked it open.

"Your father, is he still the Vicar at St. Andrews?"

"He... they... would have never understood." She wiped her nose with the back of her sleeve and closed her eyes, tears forming on the end of her long, dark lashes.

"Did Sophie know?" Lewis asked.

"Of course not," she scoffed. "We had spent a drunken night together in my room, during fresher's week. It meant nothing to her, but to me... to me, it was everything. It showed me who I really was. To her it was just something that *happened*."

"So, Sophie wasn't gay?" Graham asked.

"No. After that, she had a string of boyfriends and flings. It killed me. I was not exactly subtle with my affection, either. But it was always one way. She laughed it off most of the time."

Graham and Lewis shared a look, and Lewis nodded in silent agreement. Graham turned back to Isabelle, his voice much softer now.

"If I can ask you once more, was she seeing anyone at the time of her disappearance?"

There was a long silence.

Eventually Isabelle spoke, but her voice was barely a whisper. "Yes. Yes, she was seeing someone."

"Did you ever get a look at him? Or a name perhaps?" Lewis asked.

"A name, no. But I did see him once, through the curtains. Smug bastard knew I was watching too."

"Could you describe him for us? And was this on the night she disappeared?"

"It wasn't no, I was at work that night, but from what I remember, she was planning on seeing him again. He was tall, slim, late twenties maybe. He had long hair, dark, but it was tied up I think."

Graham clutched his pen hard between his fingers. Hard enough that the cheap biro snapped like a twig under his hands.

Just a coincidence, he thought.

She took another long draw on her cup and sat the empty back down on the table. The tension in her face softened, as though she had unloaded a great burden by speaking to the pair in that room.

"I've never told anyone," she said. "No one knows the real me."

"Miss Turner, thank you so much. You've been a great help to us today. I know it hasn't been easy."

"You're welcome," she replied, once again wiping her nose.

"If we can just ask you one more question. Did you by any chance see what car this man was driving?"

"A black Volvo. He picked her up that night in a black Volvo."

"How the hell did you know she was in love with her?" Lewis asked as the two detectives waved Isabelle out of the main doors.

"I didn't. I just remember her. She was so broken up at the time, understandable, I know, but it was how she was. She was grieving like a lover. It was when I re-read that her father was a minister that a light bulb went off. That maybe she could have been withholding information for a reason."

"Shit, we could have done with that at the time."

"Definitely. And maybe that is half her problem now, guilt. She will have to live with that for the rest of her life."

Graham pulled back the sleeve of his tweed jacket and checked the time on his wristwatch, deciding on the spot that he would need to invest in a new one.

Piece of crap, he thought.

"Can you write this up, and we'll get Morgan up to speed later?"

"Sure, what's up?"

"I've got this bloody meal tonight; I was going to pop out

and get something new to wear, but I won't be long. I'm sure as hell he'd want to hear this."

Lewis scoffed. "Yeah, no worries, mate, send me a photo from the changing room."

GRAHAM PATTED him on the shoulder playfully as he turned for the main doors and laughed aloud. "Don't be a twat, Lewis."

26

£22.99 for a bloody steak, Graham thought, as he sat there, flicking absently through a menu later that evening.

Quite out of character for him, he was early – particularly early. And as luck would have it, the table that Elena's boyfriend – *Jackson*; he should call him by his name if he were going to make this work – had booked, was available half an hour before their slot. So at least he was not standing at the bar on his own for too long. He sat, glass of still water at his side, watching people go about their evening, and waited.

He was feeling good, fresh and, thanks to the last-minute shopping trip, he was looking good as well. He wore a sharp, well-fitted, charcoal suit jacket, under which he wore a crisp, white collarless shirt that complemented his clean-shaven jawline well. He felt eyes being drawn to him as he was making his way to the table, and for once, not for the wrong reasons. Even the waitress who had brought over the water, who had to be at least half his age, had blushed slightly when he had thanked her.

I'm going to wear this more often, he thought, smiling to himself.

When he and Lewis had filled DCI Morgan in that afternoon, regarding their conversation with Isabelle Turner, he thought his colleague was about to do somersaults. The uncharacteristic half smile on Morgan's face made his infamous moustache look like it was waving at you. It was something that had not left Graham's mind, and it made him giggle even now. Isabelle had provided at least some information they needed to confirm their suspicions that the killings were linked. They had needed that desperately, and Morgan failed miserably at hiding his delight at the fact. A positive connection between the victims to share with the team in the morning, and perhaps more importantly, to take upstairs. Graham could already hear Morgan taking credit for the idea to re-interview the girl, with Lewis and Graham receiving nothing more than a passing mention. That, and the uncomfortable sound of his tongue being shoved further and further up the arses of their bosses.

No work tonight though. Tonight I am Dad. Super-bloody-Dad, in fact, and Morgan can sodding do one.

"OH, NO AINSLEY TONIGHT, DAD?" Elena said, as she took her seat opposite him and motioned with her eyes to the empty spot at his side.

Jackson had taken her coat and was folding it neatly beside them, radiating an air of arrogance that Graham felt was directed at him. It was as though Jackson was trying to show *Daddy* that his little girl's new boyfriend was the real deal. A proper gentleman. That was much to the dismay of the other males in the room, whose partners were now scolding them with looks that translated nicely into "why don't you do things like that for me?"

"Unfortunately for me, no, she was called into work at the last minute. Cleaning up after a drug bust that got kind of messy by the sounds of it."

"A downside of the profession, I assume," Jackson said with a polite smile as he took his seat next to Elena.

"One of many," Graham replied.

So far, so good, he thought.

Graham had been relying on Ainsley to be his tag-team partner for tonight's event. She would have been someone to bounce conversational ammunition off, or to pick up the pieces when all topics of chat fell from his mind, via his ear, and went crashing down into his main course. Thank god then that Elena was in a particularly talkative mood.

"I'm loving the threads, old man," she said, pointing at him with the remains of a breadstick.

Graham ruffled the collar of his jacket and chuckled heartily.

"Well thanks, kid. This old man has still got it. And if she were here, Ainsley would not be able to keep her hands to herself, if you know what I mean."

Elena raised an eyebrow, shot a look at Jackson while feigning putting her fingers down her throat, and the group erupted into laughter.

"A little too much information, Dad."

"May I ask how work has been, Mr Walker?" Jackson asked when the giggles had finally died down.

"Please, it's Graham. And good, as a matter of fact, we've had a few significant breakthroughs with the case."

He watched Jackson's reaction intently. He already knew subconsciously that he'd give nothing away, if he did in fact have anything to give, especially not in front of Elena. Part of him couldn't accept that he was even considering his daughter's boyfriend as a potential suspect. The other part, however, hoped that his face had not shown the shock he had felt at Jackson's question. He was here to make peace with the guy, to enjoy, and attempt to have a pleasant evening with his daughter and her partner. But his stomach would not let his feelings lie.

After all, there is no such thing as a coincidence.

The waitress who arrived to take their order gave Elena a look that said, "lucky girl", and swung her hips provocatively as she left. Just in case one of the men was watching, and was interested. Her smokey eyes had glared at the two men when they were reciting their individual orders; she stared with a sexual intensity and gave an image of a young woman who was on the prowl, hungry, and she didn't care who knew.

"Wow," Graham said as the waitress was just out of ear shot.

"Really, Dad?" Elena scolded him with her eyes. "Are you really going to play the part of the middle-aged misogynist?"

"Well, no. I just thought she was nice," Graham said with a smile that he directed at Jackson.

"Not my type," he replied, and kissed Elena gently on the cheek.

Yeah, of course fucking not, Graham thought. *Note to self, banter does not work.*

"You seeing Ainsley later, Dad?"

"Yeah hoping—" Graham's reply was disrupted by the loud vibration of Jackson's phone on the table.

"My apologies," he said, checking his watch. "I completely forgot, but I have to dash."

"What, like right now?" Elena asked, bemusement on her face.

"I'm sorry. I'll call you in the morning. Have a lovely evening, both of you. I'm sure it won't be a problem for your dad to give you a lift home?"

"Yeah, it's fine, kid."

Jackson got up quickly and put on his jacket, kissing Elena softly as he rose.

"I'll see you later."

Without a second thought, or a glance behind, he made his way across the restaurant and out of the entrance door. Elena, still looking confused, turned to her father and gave him an awkward smile.

"Again? Does he do this all the time?" Graham said, looking just as puzzled as his daughter.

"Leave suddenly and without warning? He has once or twice, but never during dinner."

"Yeah, because that's not weird."

"He... he's just a bit different."

"I can see that. And, what's this?"

Graham motioned to a napkin that was positioned in front of where Jackson had been seated. It looked as though he had been doodling on it during their conversation. Graham turned it so that he could get a better look. The drawing was of a cartoon girl. A cartoon girl with the head of a smiling cow. And underneath it was written a single word. Elena.

"Now that he does do," Elena said, spying the cartoon. "He loves to reimagine people as animals. That's kind of his signature thing."

"Have you seen any of his other work?"

The waitress interrupted as Elena was about to reply. Neither had seen her standing there, towering above them and smiling like a lunatic. "Steak, well done?"

"That's me," Graham said, startled. "But I'm just going to run for a leak, just put it anywhere."

"So you're leaving me as well?"

"I'll be back in a second."

Elena turned to the waitress and said, "The plant burger is for me," with an awkward grin.

HE HAD TO BE WRONG. For Elena's sake, he had to be wrong. The guy was a little strange, that was a given, but that did not make him a killer. The similarities with Isabelle Turner's description? Perhaps nothing more than an unhappy coincidence this time. But the drawing too? He had not always been right. Why then, was he heading towards the window next to the entrance door? Why, then, was every fibre of his being telling him that this man was dangerous? He would not see what he was hoping not to, when he pulled back the blind and glared out into the frosty night.

Graham poised his fingers on the edge of a blind slat. His heart was racing, and under his crisp new clothes he had begun to sweat. He closed his eyes and slowed his breathing.

I'm wrong. There will be nothing. Especially not...

He re-opened his eyes as he pulled back the blind.

THE TAILLIGHTS OF A BLACK VOLVO.

27

GRAHAM LAY in bed that night, with Ainsley tucked dutifully under one of his arms, and stared blankly at the ceiling. They had made love, and the sex was satisfying, but he could not switch off, regardless.

One coincidence I could have just about understood, but this? This is too much, even for me.

Sensing his apprehension, she turned and asked him what was wrong, and reluctantly, he told her. He told her everything.

"Jesus, Gray, you need to report this," she said when he had finished, her wide eyes piercing through the darkness, pleading with him.

"And say what? Oh, Steve, by the way, I think my daughter's new boyfriend is our killer. What do I think of him? Creepy, bit of an oddball. Wish he wasn't shagging my daughter, that's for sure. Any evidence? Nope, nothing concrete, all circumstantial, oh but the feeling in my gut says I'm right."

"Not in those words perhaps, you sarcastic git, but if there is even the smallest of chances it's him…"

"It's Elena I'm worried about."

He turned to her, and even under the dull glow of the streetlight from behind the curtains, she could see the vulnerability in his eyes. She could sense it, hear it in his voice, and it scared her.

"If I'm right, I may lose her to him, and if I'm wrong…"

"Graham…"

"I'll lose her to him, anyway. I need to be sure, Ainz. I can't go head on into this one and fuck everything up again."

"And how are you going to do that?"

"I… have some ideas."

"Do you wish to share them with me?"

He leaned in and kissed her on the forehead, pulling her tightly into his chest. Her hair smelt of coconut and cinnamon, and he inhaled deeply as he hugged her, his fingers finding hers.

"Not even remotely," he said softly. "This is on me."

"I'd be lying if I said I was not a tad concerned at that."

If superpowers or magic had really existed, then the intensity in Graham's eyes, his fixed stare, would have burned a hole straight through the ceiling, through the attic space and roof tiles, and out into the frosty night above. He spoke slowly, deliberately, and he hung on every word in turn.

"Don't be. I've got this."

HER SHIFT HAD FINISHED SLIGHTLY LATER than normal that evening. Perhaps coffee and sugar laced treats were in high demand in the waning hours of the night, or perhaps her boss was keeping her back to have her to himself.

No chance of that, I'm afraid, bucko. This one's mine.

A few of them left through the entrance doors together. He got a good look at her manager, and quickly confirmed to himself what a squidgy insect of a man he truly was. With his sweaty, chubby fingers groping around her, and his beady little eyes following her arse at every turn. Jackson had seen him in the café, undressing her with his eyes as she spoke to customers and served them their drinks. He was almost sure that he had seen him trying to hide an erection once when he had watched her bending forward while cleaning tables.

And they think I'm the monster.

Although she was always rejecting his public advances, laughed them off playfully, she looked like she enjoyed the attention and was clearly aware when his eyes were on her. Perhaps she even encouraged it. He had his suspicions, but a quick check of her unsurprisingly public social media accounts by James confirmed it. She appeared to be what Elena would have called, *a little bit of a slut.*

Still, this one will be fun.

Although apparently keenly aware of when she was being ogled at, she was not the most observant of creatures. He had been following her, at a not so discreet distance, for a few days now since she had agreed to a date. A date, he noted, with someone whose first name was the only information she knew. She had not appeared to have noticed his presence at all. Not outside her work, not near her university halls, not in the pub, not even as she lay asleep in bed.

. . .

Sure Elena, she's not you, but that's the point. She looks great on the outside, I will admit, but she's hollow, and not a fine, fully rounded specimen like yourself. I'm sure someone will miss her, and I'm sure that sad excuse who calls himself her boss will have one more pity wank before the funeral, but honestly, she is just like the rest. Just a pair of tits and a waste of fucking oxygen. And we will be better off without her.

28

"Yes, of course, nine-thirty will be fine. I'll see you then, thanks."

Graham hung up the phone, picked up his favourite mug from the kitchen counter, and drank deeply from his morning coffee. It tasted sweet on his tongue, and the feeling of invigoration forming behind his eyes from the caffeine was most welcome. The sun had been up for well over an hour, but a low, heavy mist still lingered in the little garden beyond his kitchen window. He shivered, and considered adding another layer, perhaps his faithful khaki fleece, to his chosen outfit for the day. For now, that could wait, however, as he had another call to make.

"Morgan, sir, it's Graham. Yeah, not too bad, look, listen, I'm feeling like shit this morning... vomiting from both ends if you know what I mean, so I'm afraid I won't be in today... Yeah, I've already spoken to Lewis, he knows the score...

Yeah, the meetings are going okay, I'll be honest it's not exactly a party, but I definitely think it is helping... Okay great, thank you sir... I'll try, bye sir."

Ainsley left work only half an hour ago. She was still asking questions, still probing, even as she walked out the door into the brisk morning chill. She had threatened, multiple times in fact, to go to Steve Morgan herself and tell him what Graham had told her. But with some persuasion, and a flutter of his eyelashes, that he had promised never to repeat, she had given him a couple of days to get some evidence. Some *real* evidence. She did not like it one bit. That was clear from the stony expression on her face as he had kissed her goodbye. And she had almost turned the air blue with all the names she had called him that morning. But at least he had a couple of days.

He drained the coffee and sat the mug in the sink.

"Game face, old man," he told himself. "You know what to do."

"GOOD MORNING, sir, and welcome to Southeast Vehicle Rentals. How may I help you today?"

"Yeah hi, the name's Walker. I have a car reserved for this morning."

The lady behind the counter smiled as she turned and entered something on the keyboard of her computer. She was not a traditionally attractive woman, not in Graham's mind at least, but he noted she had kind, blue eyes that complemented her soft features well. She reminded him a little of his own mother. Even the way she sat brought back memories of the woman who had raised him, and who had been gone now for many years.

"That's right, I have a Mondeo for you, all ready to go out front. Just need to see your driver's licence and take a swipe of your credit card as well, please. It has a half a tank of fuel in it, and we would appreciate it if it was returned as so."

"Yep, no worries."

She took his documentation and took it to the rear of the office to photocopy. Returning to her screen then, she hummed a pretty little tune as she typed, finally handing over the key with a wide smile when she was done.

"Going anywhere nice then, sir?"

"I am, as it happens. And I'm quite looking forward to it."

THE BUILDING where Jackson Page worked, a two-storey, glass-fronted building of modern design, was situated just one street back from Cardiff bay. The morning had remained relatively dry, as the man on the weather last night had promised, and the last of the morning mist had lifted. As a result, the bay was alive with activity. Locals heading to work bustled with tourists rushing to get a photo of the Senedd and the city's waterfront. This at least helped to obscure Graham's rental car, parked on the road opposite Jackson's building, even if it did nothing for his nerves. He wound down the window, tossing the "No Smoking" sign into the street and between the feet of the revellers, and lit a cigarette.

Where are you?

Where he, *Jackson*, was, was behind a desk on the ground floor, typing away on a keyboard and looking way too fucking normal for Graham's liking. He was smiling at everyone as they walked by, making small talk, and laughing at people's jokes. When he got up to make a cup of tea, it could have been coffee, he took one each to the people working in his immediate vicinity.

Glad Lewis can't see this, he would get far too many ideas.

MINUTES TURNED INTO HOURS, and more than once, Graham had to flash his police identification at a passing traffic warden to avoid getting a ticket. He didn't know what he was expecting to see if he was honest, but the whole heap of normal he had witnessed that morning was not it.

As lunch time approached, and as Graham hastily shoved the remaining half of a sandwich that he had bought from a petrol station into his mouth, Jackson left the building. Graham almost missed it. Swearing, and throwing what was left of his lunch into the footwell of the car, he snatched the driver's door open, pulled the hood of his jacket up over the peak of his baseball cap, and followed on foot.

He maintained a careful distance, peering up from beneath his dark cap only to confirm the direction, and distance to, his target. He was breathing heavily, sweat was pooling on the band of the hat, and his stomach was rife with butterflies. At one point, he feared the petrol station ploughman's would appear on the concrete below. But he held it together.

Graham was not a particularly small man, but he weaved between the crowds with all the grace of a trained assassin. Not once drawing attention to himself. And as far as he could tell, not once letting his prey know that he was being followed.

Where are you going, creep? he thought, as Jackson approached a church with towering double doors.

He hung back, tucked just behind a phone box, and watched him enter the church from a smaller door off to the side. Graham stood poised to strike, the mist of his hot breath carried off in the early afternoon breeze. He stood there and considered a thousand possibilities as to why Jackson had gone there, and if he should burst in, confront him, and make him confess to his crimes.

Don't be too hasty, old man.

The heavy double doors swung open. First the left, and then the right. Jackson appeared and Graham rubbed his eyes. He had no real expectations as to what he might see, but that was not remotely close to what he had thought. Jackson was wearing an apron and carrying a chalk-board sign.

What the hell?

Jackson placed the sign down and positioned it so it could be read clearly from the across the street, smiling up at the world as he did. Shaking his head in disbelief, Graham lowered his hood, took the hat from his head, and wiped his sodden brow with the back of his hand.

Now that I did not see coming, he thought, reading the sign.

In large, clear white letters it read simply, "Soup Kitchen – Open."

Graham's thoughts were then interrupted by the vibrations originating in his trouser pocket. He reached in with a gloved hand and retrieved his damaged phone.

Incoming call – Elena.

Shit, he thought, pulling off a glove with his teeth and sliding one of his fingers across the cracked screen.

"Dad, are you okay? I've just spoken to Lewis in the office, and he said you're sick."

"Yeah, I'm fine, kid, don't worry."

"Where are you? I can hear traffic."

"Oh, umm... I'm out in the garden." He winced at the words. He hated lying to her.

"Yeah... sure, anyway, are you still meeting me in town later? To get Lewis' birthday present, and pay the deposit at the rugby club for the party?"

Fuck, I forgot that was today.

He shot a glance up, and the sign now stood alone on the pavement. It was as if the kindhearted and well-meaning message displayed on it, written in chalk in a careful hand, was intended as a direct "F-you" to him. But that was insane, wasn't it?

"Yeah, I'll be there," he eventually replied.

"I'll be finished up in work by about two-ish. Meet you in the café at about three? Grab a late lunch before we head in?"

"Sounds great, kid. I'll see you then."

Graham hung up the phone, returning it to his pocket as he glared at the towering gothic structure before him. He turned, breaking his gaze only at the last second, and made his way, defeated, back down the street towards the car.

JACKSON PEERED, with a cold grimace from beyond the immense oak doors, his form hidden by shadows cast from the ancient holy gateway. He could see clearly from here, out into the daylight, and to the street beyond.

The hooded figure that had been stalking him through the city that afternoon turned and walked away. He'd had an inkling as to who it could have been. And he was right.

I would have expected you to have been more careful, Detective Inspector.

.   .   .

HE DREW a slender finger down the back of the door and tapped gently on the aged, pitted wood, not for one second taking his gaze from the man retreating down the street. He drew a slow breath, and smiled a crooked smile.

29

September 27th 2018, 18:10

"A pint of mild, and an orange juice and lemonade please, mate," Graham said, motioning to the barman with a twenty-pound note.

"Ice in the OJ?"

"Aye, go on. And I'll have two bags of those nuts as well, please."

The pub was busy for a mid-week evening, and Graham and Lewis were lucky to get their favourite seats in a booth by the door. The low hum of chatter hung in the air, which itself was heavy with the smell of stale alcohol and Chinese food from the takeaway next door. The stools by the bar were, as usual, occupied by the regulars who could have been there since lunchtime. And judging by the swaying on a few, some perhaps even earlier. The remaining small tables and booths that adorned the rest of the pub, all bar a few, were full to the brim as well. Friends meeting after work. Groups of girls getting oiled before heading into town. The odd tourist cramming a final drink in before the train journey home.

Lewis had been hesitant to attend what he felt was an off the cuff and all too random pint in the local the day before his birthday. Graham had convinced him otherwise and persuaded him a drink was in his best interests. But as with most things he planned, Graham had an ulterior motive that extended beyond cheap lager, stale crisps and a hearty chat.

The worn leather of the booth whimpered under the denim of Graham's jeans as he slid across it, and he passed the glass of murky beer across the polished mahogany table to Lewis with a smile.

"Top man, thanks," Lewis said, taking a generous gulp of the frothy beverage.

"You're more than welcome." Graham raised his glass. "To good health, mate."

Lewis returned the gesture. "And you, cheers. So, are you going to tell me what was up with you yesterday?"

Opening a bag of salty nuts, and cramming a handful into his mouth, Graham replied, "I had the shits, Lew."

"I know you better than that, old man."

He swallowed the nuts and sighed. "Yeah, I suppose you do. Look, there is something. If I'm right, it could bring this case to a swift end."

"So go on then, tell me."

"No, not yet. I still need to confirm a few things, but I will, I promise. After the weekend, hopefully. Let's get your birthday out of the way first."

"My birthday? Jesus Christ, that feels like the last thing we should be thinking about with everything going on. Maybe we give it a miss this year."

"I agree. But it will be quiet. I promise. Nothing like last time."

Graham laughed into his drink.

Lewis smirked. "I don't want any male strippers, or female strippers, for that matter. Just keep it clean this time, for god's sake. The photos still pop up on friends' socials from time to time, and to this day they still make me feel queasy."

Graham burst into a fit of laughter at the memory of his partner blind drunk on his birthday the year before, tied to a lamppost, with a stripper's underwear dangling from his open, dribbling mouth. A number of the other party attendees had posed in front of him for photographs, many of which found their way on to social media the morning after. Detective Chief Inspector Morgan had not been best pleased, and had given Lewis perhaps the only telling off he had ever received in his life, definitely the only one of his police career.

"You just have to promise to follow my every command, starting the moment we clock out of work tomorrow."

Lewis put his pint down on a bar mat, closed his eyes and shook his head, smiling. "You're serious?"

"Absolutely, mate. Trust me."

Graham composed himself, wiping a tear from his reddened face, and was about to offer to get another round of drinks in, when there was an almighty crash from behind them. One of the regulars, a burly man in his late forties, had thrown another, much younger and smaller man, across the pub and on top of a table where a group of young girls were sitting. He had taken all but one of the glasses with him on his way to the floor, but he got to his feet quickly, and threw a punch at the larger man. His fist connected, and the burly regular smashed backwards into the bar, saliva and blood spraying from his mouth and coating the collar of his shirt. Graham and Lewis were on their feet in an instant, heading over to break up the brawl.

"Stay out of it, you," said the second man as he shoved Lewis to one side.

Graham stepped in and tried to restrain him, only to receive a punch to the side of the head that had been originally destined for the other man.

"C'mon then," the burly man said, gesturing to everyone in the room. "No one stares at my bird's tits and gets away with it. I'll 'ave the lot of you."

Too preoccupied with puffing out his chest and threatening everyone in sight, the larger of the two men did not see the barman coming, nor did he see the pool cue he was carrying. He fell to the ground like a wrecking ball, hitting the carpet with a sickening thud.

"You," the barman said, pointing to the man that had shoved Lewis. "The police have been called, so you had better fuck off if you don't wanna get nicked. And don't come back neither, you and your mates are all banned."

The man scarpered quickly out of the door; his friends, who had been watching from the sidelines, quickly followed. The barman turned to Lewis, and a slightly dazed Graham, put the pool cue on the bar, and returned to a comforting grin.

"Sorry about that, lads. Those two prats have been sizing each other up all evening. I was waiting for it all to kick off. Thanks for your help. Can I get you two anything?"

"No worries," Graham replied, rubbing his head and offering the barman a weary smile. "Another round would be great though, thanks."

. . .

A LITTLE LATER THAT EVENING, after a few less-exciting drinks, Graham and Lewis shared their goodbyes on the front step of the pub. They laughed once again about the night's antics and had promised to talk about it some more the next day. Graham stood and watched his partner, his best friend, climb into a taxi and drive off into the chilly night. His admiration and respect, hell, his love for Lewis, was only growing stronger. And he could think of no other person he would rather have at his side. He allowed himself a smile as he took out his phone and dialled Elena's number.

"All sorted, kid. Lewis has agreed to follow any instructions I give him, so getting him to the party shouldn't be a problem."

"Is Ainsley coming up with you?"

"She's working a little late, so I think she's coming straight from work and meeting us there. What about you, want me to pick you up?"

"Jackson is picking me up, so I'll meet you there if that's cool?"

Graham stared at the ground, hiding his anger behind clenched teeth.

That fucking boy, he thought.

"Of course, I'll see you then. Just... just be careful, Elena."

"I'm always careful," she said with a laugh. "Love you, Dad. I'll see you tomorrow."

"You sure will, love you too, kid."

He returned the phone to his pocket, rubbing his hands together for warmth as the hot breath from his nose dispersed like white smoke on the evening breeze.

. . .

"Love you too."

30

ELENA DANCED across the polished wooden floor of her bedroom from her en-suite bathroom, wearing nothing but a towel and a toothy smile. The music swelled and filled the comfortable space as she twirled and leapt like a half-naked ballerina across the bare timbers. She reached the bed, and bowed in thanks to her captive audience of stuffed animals, letting out a hearty laugh as she threw herself across the duvet. The night was going to be wonderful; she could feel it. She had been helping her dad prepare for Lewis' birthday, and although it was only a small affair, the excitement of having all of her favourite people in one place filled her, and she found it impossible to hold back a permanent grin.

She reached for her phone, which was on charge and lay on the small table to the side of her bed, and kicked her legs in the air like an overexcited schoolgirl as she dialled Jackson's number.

"Alright handsome, it's me," she said.

"Hello. It's great to hear your voice."

"I know. It is rather beautiful." She laughed. "Hurry your pretty little arse up, I want to get there first to make sure everything is spot on before they all get there."

"Elena. I'm sorry."

Her smile quickly faded and was replaced by the stony glare of a woman scorned. "Oh god, what now?"

"Something has come up. It shouldn't take all evening; I'll have to meet you there a little later."

"Are you kidding me?" she said. "You're telling me this now, why?"

"It's just a work thing."

"Jacks, you draw kids' stuff, you're not a fucking life-guard, what could have possibly come up?"

"You're being silly."

"Don't call me silly."

"Stupid then. I won't be long. And I'll make it up to you. I promise."

She managed a half smile but quickly withdrew it, picking up a teddy bear and throwing it across the room.

"I'll be the judge of that," she snapped. "Look, just don't be too late. I don't want to be standing around on my own like a lemon."

"Scout's honour, you won't even notice I'm not there. I'll call you later when I'm on my way."

"Yeah, alright. Speak to you later then, dickhead."

Elena threw her phone back towards the table without looking. It missed, and tumbled on to the floor. All the joy drained from her face, and she sat staring out of her bedroom window as dark clouds gathered in the distance. The phone call had left a bitter taste in her mouth and a hollow feeling in the pit of her stomach. She clutched a hand to the towel draped over her chest, and tears appeared in the corners of her eyes. She was scared. But as much as she searched, she did not know why.

A FEW MILES AWAY, in a mid-terrace across the city, Graham was also getting ready for the night's festivities. He was freshly showered, clean shaven, and well dressed in new dark jeans and black shirt. The smell of his new aftershave hung in the air as he poured himself a glass of lemonade, and sat it on the table as he pulled out his phone.

New message – Lewis.

As I said yesterday, mate, you have to follow my instructions to the tee. I promise you there is gold at the end of this rainbow. G

He pressed send and then checked the time.

"Oh shit, I better get going."

He put the phone on the table next to the glass and rushed towards the bathroom to brush his teeth and check his reflection in the mirror one last time. He was clearly confident that his plan for the night would work, and he pushed his troubles and the case to the back of his mind. He was so fixated on what he was doing that he did not notice the figure lurking beyond the kitchen window.

There was a sound of metal on metal as the lock was picked. The handle fell, and the back door swung open silently. A tall figure, dressed head to toe in black, entered the kitchen. It stood still and listened. Content that Graham was upstairs, it advanced into the house, closing the door behind it. It looked around the room once, and then again, finding Graham's drink on the table. With a gloved hand, it took from its pocket a tiny vial of white powder. It emptied the contents into the glass and retreated into the shadows to watch.

Graham bolted down the stairs and pulled on his shoes.

He noticed a cold patch of air as he moved towards the kitchen, but looking up, he saw that the windows and door were all closed.

This house is fucking haunted, I swear.

He turned for the front door, draining the glass of lemonade in one as he passed the table. As he reached for the front door, he patted the pockets of his jeans, realising that his phone was still on the table.

As he turned on the spot, his vision blurred. He put his hands to his face and rubbed, but it only made things worse. With each step, his balance deteriorated until he fell to his knees and vomited. Graham hit the floor face first, splitting his lip open on the bare wood of the living room. He could taste blood mixed with the remains of his lunch on his tongue, and he tried in vain to get up. The last thing he saw, through the blur of the kitchen doorway, was a pair of black boots walking towards him.

The man, dressed in black, flipped Graham over and crouched over his limp, unconscious body. He breathed slowly, deeply, and with purpose. He bent closer, putting his face only a few inches from Graham's.

"She's mine, old man," Jackson said. "We *will* be together, and nobody, especially not you, will get in our way."

He stood and glared disapprovingly at the man at his feet, the man now at his will. He reached a gloved hand into his waistband and produced a long, slender knife. And with a twisted, toothy grin, he rubbed the flat of the blade across Graham's face and throat.

"You really are kind of pathetic, are you not, Mr. Walker?"

Graham's phone, still on the table, vibrated and broke

Jackson's gaze. He stood and took the damaged mobile in his hand.

New message – Lewis.

I'm all yours, mate, do with me what you please lol, L.

An evil grin shot across the man's face, and his breathing elevated as he flicked through the messages.

Now that is interesting, he thought.

He returned the knife to its sheath and leaned down to pat Graham on the shoulder, whispered in his ear, his hot breath kissing Graham on the cheek.

"As fate would have it, it seems that today is not *your* day. A new game has presented itself to me. And oh, how I do love a good game, Mr. Walker."

Jackson retraced his steps to the back door, turning just as he reached the threshold, once again grinning at Graham's motionless body.

"Take care of yourself, Graham," he said with a chuckle. "I'll be seeing you and your beautiful daughter soon."

THE TINY RUGBY club bar was packed shoulder to shoulder. It seemed as though the whole of South Wales Police was in attendance, and then some. The hum of chatter, mixed with the awful eighties' songs coming from the jukebox, was almost deafening, and Elena had to strain to hear DCI Morgan talk.

"I said, have you heard from your father?" the detective chief inspector asked.

"Not yet," she replied. "I've tried his phone but he's not picking up."

"No sign of Lewis Reed either?"

"I've not seen him, sorry."

Ainsley interrupted them, crashing through the main doors, soaking wet, and struggling with her umbrella.

"So, it's raining, then," Ainsley said sarcastically as Elena rushed to help her with the unwieldy brolly.

"Ainsley, have you spoken to Dad?"

"Not since this afternoon, darling, why?"

Ainsley could see the worry in the green pools of Elena's eyes. She took her by the hand and pulled her to one side.

"Elena, what's going on?"

"It's probably nothing. They, him and Lewis, I mean, have probably stopped for a drink on the way. It's just...it's just he's not normally late. Not to things like this, anyway."

"I'm sure they're fine."

Elena searched Ainsley's face, and then glared deeply, unblinking, into her eyes. "Then why do I feel sick?"

"YOU'RE NORMALLY one for an adventure, Gray, but this is taking the piss," Lewis said to himself, struggling to see far beyond the windscreen of his car.

It was dark on the mountain roads, very dark, and the heavens had opened some time ago now. Lewis could barely see the road in his headlights between the frantic swaying of the car's wiper blades. He pulled the car into a layby and checked the maps on his phone.

Still going the right way, wherever the fuck that is.

He had received a message from Graham's phone, just a postcode and the words *"See you soon."* He had thought little of it, but the further he drove into the darkness, the more he questioned his friend's sanity.

This is bloody suicide.

He pulled the car back onto the road and continued,

holding his phone to his ear as he drove. It went straight to answerphone.

"Graham, you are a bloody idiot. If I plummet off a cliff for some half-assed party with a fat stripper and a warm pint, I'll kill you myself." He threw the phone onto the passenger's seat, shaking his head.

After what seemed like an eternity, and several close shaves with the local sheep, the satellite navigation burst into life.

"In one-hundred and fifty yards, the destination is on your left."

A stone cottage loomed into view in Lewis' headlights, with a black car parked in its driveway. The cottage was dilapidated. It looked as though no one had lived there in years. The whitewashed paint was peeling, and in several places had fallen off entirely. Two of the four windows were boarded up, and there was a gaping hole in the slate-tiled roof. What would have once been a beautiful garden was now an overgrown jungle of long grasses and thick thorny bushes. A dim light flickered in one of the windows.

What the sodding hell am I doing here?

"Graham?" Lewis called as he stepped from the comfort of the car and into night. The rain was beating and bouncing off the roof of the car as the wind howled and whipped at the lapels of his jacket.

"Graham?"

Lewis reached the front door and pushed it open with a shove. Silence.

"Graham, where the fuck are you?" he called down the dank hallway.

Water from the open roof had made its way through the ceiling and was pooling in the entrance way, where fungi were now growing on the carpets and peeling wallpaper.

The air was cold, thick with the smell of moss and vegetation. A chill ran up the length of Lewis' spine as he made his way down the hall, using his phone as a torch. His heart was in his throat, and he heard a crash from beyond a closed door at the end of the hall, and he could see light escaping from beneath the frame.

"Graham, is that you? Hello?"

He reached his hand out to grab the handle. He held it in his hand for a long moment, considering what lay beyond. His heart was pounding in his ears, and he could feel the adrenalin building, racing through his veins. He pushed the door open and froze in terror.

What lay beyond the door was no party. Someone had propped a young woman's body against the far wall in a sitting position, legs splayed apart. She was completely naked, apart from a name tag that had been pierced through her left nipple. It simply read, "Becky." A tattered blue backpack lay on the floor to her left.

Lewis fought off the feeling to vomit as he stepped over the threshold, one hand covering his mouth. There was so much blood. Her hands were bound and held above her head by a hook on the wall. She had been beaten, badly, he thought. The cause of death was most likely the deep wound on her neck that stretched from one side to the other. Her toned, naked form was stained red from the throat down. He took another step forward to see her more clearly, his boot stuck to the slate-tiled floor, stuck in Becky's congealed life force.

What the fuck happened here?

"Graham?" he called out once more as his voice trembled.

The door behind him slammed shut, and he turned and saw a blackened figure.

"Graham?"

Before he could react, he was struck on the head. Lewis hit the slate tile hard, face first. He landed in a lake of blood. His blood and hers. He was turned over. Blood dripped in his eyes, and he could barely make out the figure now standing over him, but he could see the blade in his hand, and the pig mask that covered its face.

"HAPPY BIRTHDAY, DETECTIVE."

31

THUMP, thump, thump.

"Ah, my head," Graham said as he opened his eyes.

The light from the living room pendant was blinding, and he covered his eyes with a bloody palm, his back in agony from spending the night on the hard floor of his living room.

How the hell am I here? Why am I on the floor? Graham struggled to sit up.

His thoughts were muddled and his throat was dry. The fact that he had placed a hand in a pile of congealed vomit as he rose, his own vomit, did not cross his mind twice. He looked up towards the kitchen, and to his surprise, saw the first rays of morning sunlight streaming through the window.

Thump, thump, thump. The banging continued.

He had no recollection of the events that led to him

being on the floor. The last thing he remembered was getting ready to leave, then turning back to get his...

My phone.

He stood, and with jelly legs, made his way over to the dining room table. His phone was not there. With his fingers, he rubbed his forehead, which felt as though it was about to split apart, and took a seat. He could still taste the blood from his split lip, and his throat burned from throwing up.

Thump, thump, thump. The banging was coming from the front door.

"Fuck me, I'm coming," he called out.

He made his way to the front door and ripped it open, the sunlight from the other side almost blinding him as the door completed its arc into its frame. Elena jumped at him through the doorway, throwing her arms around his neck, almost knocking him off balance.

"Jesus Christ," she started. "Answer your bloody phone when people call you. I've been worried sick."

"I ... I don't know where it is," he replied, still guarding his eyes.

She shook her head at him and noticed the pile of vomit on the floor, her face letting on that she had come to her own conclusion.

"Guessing by the state on you, and this place, I would say that you had your own party here. No wonder you didn't make it to the club. Bit pissed off that you've been drinking though, Dad, you were doing so well." Her eyes flashed with disappointment.

"No...no... I haven't been drinking, I swear. I don't know what happened."

"Bullshit. So come on then, where is he?"

"Where's who?" he asked, completely bemused.

"Lewis. He's here with you, right? He didn't make an appearance last night either."

"What? No, I haven't seen him since we left the station yesterday."

The pair looked hard at each other for a long moment, neither yet comprehending the full implications of the conversation they were having. Elena could see that her father's mind was currently mush, and he could not fully look her in the eyes. She wondered whether it was because he could not focus his vision, or if it had something to do with the terrible foreboding in the pit of her stomach. She finally lifted her head, put a hand on his shoulder and managed a tense smile.

"Sit yourself down, Dad, I'll put the kettle on."

THE HOT WATER cascaded down his back and washed away the previous night's events. Not the memory of it. No, that would stay with him until the end of his days. The screams. The endless pleading and the fear from their eyes. That was his. But the shower washed the grime, the dirt, and the sweat down the drain. He slid open the glass door, wiped the steam from the mirror, and gazed at his own naked form, smiling back at him. Jackson Page dressed himself in his usual smart attire and gave himself an extra spray of aftershave. He had earned that much, after all.

He laid a towel on the ground and knelt beside his freshly made bed, reaching under to remove the loose floorboard from its perch. He had some new friends for his existing residents to play with, and he could not wait to introduce them.

The coffee was hot. It burned as it trickled down his

throat, but the rush of caffeine invigorated him. He exhaled and looked to the horizon beyond the full height windows.

"Good morning," he said with a smile.

He drained the cup and placed it in the sink, filling it with water as he pulled his phone out of his pocket.

New message – Elena.

Sorry about last night, babe, things got a bit out of hand. Let's do lunch. J xxx

I cannot wait to hear about your night, he thought, strolling for the door with a spring in his step.

THE TOAST SAT cold and uneaten on the plate beside the window. The butter had congealed on the side, and the jar of jam sat to its left, unopened. Only the mug of strong black coffee was empty, and that sat on the table next to Graham's elbow. Elena sat across from him, sipping her tea, occasionally looking up from her phone to glare at her father with disapproving and disappointed eyes. To her, he was nursing yet another hangover in the long line of "last times". The reality, although she did not believe it, was vastly different. What it was to Graham himself, however, was still a mystery.

The only certain thing, the only solid fact of the morning, was that Lewis was missing and not answering his phone. His parents had not heard from him, Elena had checked, although she had ended the call on a lighthearted note so as not to alarm them. She had said that he had probably got lucky and was in bed with a beautiful blonde somewhere, sleeping off the night. Lewis had not called into work either, like he did on some of his days off to catch up on paperwork. Graham had struggled with the operation of his house phone, in the absence of his mobile, to confirm that fact. Now they both sat in silence, each considering hugely distinct possibilities.

"You need to phone Ainsley, Dad, let her know you're not in a ditch," Elena said after a long few minutes of silence.

He rubbed his forehead frantically with the tips of his fingers and sighed. "Yeah, I will, kid, just not right now. I probably sound exactly how I feel."

"And look," she added coldly.

"Exactly."

She put her cup down and played with one of her white-gold dreadlocks, looking at the ground like an uneasy child as she did.

"If you weren't drinking last night…"

"I wasn't—"

"If," she cut him off. "Then how the hell do you explain all of this?"

Graham looked out of the kitchen window to the tiny garden beyond and shifted nervously in his seat. He closed his eyes and let out a long, drawn-out breath. He had his suspicions, but that was all they were for now, and he would keep them to himself.

"Elena, I can't."

He reached for his mug and was visibly unimpressed when he realised it was empty. He spun on the spot and flicked the kettle on.

"The last thing I remember was getting ready. I had a glass of *lemonade*, texted Lewis and was getting ready to leave. I just remember getting to the door, realising I didn't have my phone… and that's it. Nothing, until this morning."

He stared into the green pools of her eyes, the eyes of her mother, and pleaded with her to believe him. She glared back, considering, looking into his very soul, searching for the truth.

"Dad, I—" The obnoxious ringing of Graham's house-phone cut her off. He snatched the handset, put it to his ear, and let out a deep sigh.

"Lewis, that better fucking be you."

"Walker, it's Steve Morgan."

Graham bolted to his feet. His eyes were wide and what colour he had, drained from his face. His stomach flipped and his mouth was dry as he went to answer. Had he known? Deep down, had he known? He shot a look at Elena, and her face mirrored his own.

"Good morning, sir," he finally managed. "How can I help you this morning?"

"Graham, I'm going to cut the shit, save us both the niceties. The killer has struck again. At least we assume it is them."

"What... When? Where?"

"They found two bodies this morning."

"I'm sorry sir, did you say *two*?" He cupped a hand to his mouth as if not to vomit.

"I DID. And if I were you, I would get here. Sharpish."

32

THE BOY with the blue backpack, now a young man of perhaps twelve or thirteen, sat in the inky blackness of his room and waited. Lights out would not be called for another ten minutes, and there was still much activity beyond his door.

His eyes were closed, and his breathing slow and deep. He had meant to carry out his plan, his quest, for some time, and that evening all the pieces were finally falling perfectly into place. His stomach was full of butterflies, and they were making him feel sick. He had not eaten this evening, and now he wished he had. He pinched his lips to hold back the gas and bile.

Sweeping the hair from his face with a clammy hand, he opened his eyes towards the bedroom door. Footsteps. High heels chiming on the linoleum, echoing from down the hall. They stopped outside his room. Silence, followed by a single, purposeful knock.

You've got my attention.

He stood, as the footsteps faded, and kinked his neck to one side, letting out a sigh of relief as his head came back to centre with an audible click.

Tonight, she will pay dearly for all that she has done.

"YOU WANT to go to *that* car park again?" she asked in puzzlement.

"Yes," Jackson replied. "If you are going to do what you do, then at least let me choose the venue."

She didn't argue. "One knock as always, just before lights out."

He nodded silently and turned away.

As he had grown older, more mature, she had shared him around. A few close friends at first, but it was not long until some colleagues had got wind of it, of him, and wanted in.

SHE SOON REGRETTED HER DECISION. She became jealous. He was *hers*. She could not bear to imagine or witness another's hands on him. He was *hers*.

She called an end to it, threatening to expose those who opposed her, although she herself had no intention of stopping. She would have to sneak him out, hidden by the night, and take him in the shadows.

IT WAS THERE HE WAITED. It was there he planned.

Jackson pulled on his jumper and made his way out of the door. Moonlight filtered through the windows and lit sections of the otherwise pitch-black hallway with diagonal bars of shining luminescence. The air was icy, dank, and all was deathly silent. His footsteps, although light and placed with care, still echoed far into the shadows. His beating heart filled his ears, but his breathing remained deep and purposeful. He was much calmer than he expected he would have been. That was good. He had to remain in control, to remain focused.

The double doors that led to the car park creaked reluctantly into the night. In the darkness, the only thing that was visible were headlights. The piney scent of the air freshener filled his lungs as he snatched the passenger's door open, and the lit end of her cigarette floated in the darkness like a bottled firefly. And she smiled through her mouth of stained and rotting teeth.

"I was wondering if you were actually coming."

"I'm here," he replied, strapping in and facing dead forward.

"You always take that bloody tatty old bag with you everywhere, don't you?"

He kept facing front and did not answer. He was holding one strap of his bag, now in the footwell, and rubbing it frantically. She leaned over and squeezed his knee, cigarette ash dropping over his trousers. He could smell her, taste her in his mouth.

"Attaboy."

THE JOURNEY WAS PLEASANTLY quiet to begin with, although it was doubtful that she actually expected any conversation. She sang, poorly, along to country songs on the radio as they got closer to his location of choice for the evening. Whether it was to break the deafening silence, or to mask her increasing excitement, god only knows, but all he knew was that *his* breathing was getting faster. He could feel the adrenaline building in his veins, and his hands shook.

Relax, he told himself.

They turned into the forest car park, the car's headlights finding the forms of hazel, ash, and old oaks, casting their skeletal silhouettes far off into the misty gloom. A pair of ghostly eyes reflected from a nearby patch of bushes as the car rolled to a stop on the gravel.

HE COULD HEAR the change in her breathing. It was all he could hear now that the car was no longer running. Her hand was groping for him in the darkness. And found his leg.

"You are mine, boy. Remember that."

She licked the end of his ear up and down. He could feel her hot breath, tainted with putrid smoke, kissing his neck. He sat still, motionless, and kept facing forward. His hand was clutched tightly around something, and was trembling.

"How are you still scared, after all this time?" she asked, licking her teeth and sliding off her underwear. "It's only me."

She leaned towards him again, pressing her breasts at his face.

"That's why!" he screamed.

At once she recoiled in horror, the back of her head striking the driver's door window with a sickening thud. She gasped for breath, hands clawing at her throat as she coughed blood onto the windscreen. The item from his hand was now buried in her jugular. She tried to breathe, to speak, blood spraying, covering him with each curdling gargle. He stared at her, smiling, and in her eyes, she knew that this was inevitable, that this was to be her end. Her body convulsed forward one final time, and her head came to rest against the steering wheel with a crack. She became limp, motionless, but her eyes did not leave him.

IT WOULD HAVE BEEN impossible to say how long he sat in the car with his now eternally silent friend. All he knew was that the sun was rising, and the birds in the trees were singing the first verses of their morning songs as he tossed the lit match.

CLOTHES ANEW, from the inside of his tatty, blue backpack, he made his way back home through the cold, fading dawn. He would be back in bed long before anyone would be up. And his absence would have never been noticed.

33

September 29th 2018, 10:50

The car sounded about as healthy as Graham felt, as he and it wound up and down the perilous mountain roads towards the crime scene. The visibility had been abysmal. It had been raining for most of the night, and it had not yet stopped today. If his headache was not enough to obstruct his vision, then the windscreen, which had been desperate to be cleaned six months ago, and the large van in front of his car spewing up mud and gravel, would surely do the trick. Whether it was a curse or a blessing, and only he truly knew, the slow drive to the scene gave him plenty of time to digest the information he had received earlier that day.

Graham turned the old Jeep off of the main road and down a narrow track. The towering mountains, and the forest they upheld, gave way to a vast open area of bare blueish-grey rock. He got out from the car, cigarette pursed between his lips, and stood in awe at the towering smooth faces of the cliffs as they rose all around him.

"Walker," Detective Chief Inspector Morgan said, calling out from beneath the hood of his rain mac.

"Sir," he replied, nodding his head.

Graham cupped his hands around the cigarette to protect it from the wind as he lit it, and flicked the extinguished match to the ground. His eyes matched Morgan's as the other man completed his approach towards Graham's car. He could see the hive of activity further ahead, concentrated on one of the tallest faces of stone, but the SOCO tents and flood lights obscured most of his view.

"What the hell is this place?" Graham asked.

"What ... never mind that."

"Looks like an old quarry," he continued, apparently ignoring Morgan's response, and gazing around at the scene before him.

The rain fell harder, and a drop landed on the end of his cigarette, putting it out. Unfazed, he threw it to the ground, wiped the water from his face, drew another and lit it. It was as if he was in a trance. His eyes darted left and right, not fixing on a single thing for long. His eyes were searching for *him*. They were searching for Lewis.

"It *is* an old quarry," Morgan said after a long moment. "It's used by local sport climbers now; they've been bolting routes here for the past few years. Anyway, look Graham..."

Morgan sighed and looked down at the ground, clearly hesitant to continue. He wiped the rain from his moustache, pulled down his hood, and fixed Graham with an expression of deep pity and regret.

"Mate, you don't want to see this."

"No. No, Steve, I do. I have to."

Reluctantly, and with some amount of pain behind his eyes, Morgan stood to one side and allowed Graham to pass.

. . .

THE SCENE that greeted him was chaotic. People were walking and running in every direction, shouting inaudible commands back and forth at one another from beneath hoods, umbrellas, and masks. He felt as if he was crossing the space in slow motion. The rain, which had yet again intensified, crashed down on his splitting head, further adding to the air of confusion. Although, through it all, he still found her eyes. Ainsley's eyes. That, even from beneath her soaked and mud-stained uniform, portrayed a look of sheer terror that, at the same time, still appeared to be relieved to see him. She embraced him with all the energy she could muster. It had been a morning of mornings, and it was far from over yet.

"You fucking idiot," she said as she welled up, pressing her face into his sodden chest. "Where the hell were you last night? We were worried sick."

"We?"

"Yes, *we.* Me and that beautiful daughter of yours."

"Oh, it's a long story, one that I bloody well hope is in no way connected to all of this." He motioned to the scene unfolding behind them, to the ocean of bodies and activity that had now filled the quarry.

"What? Why would it be?"

He pulled her in tighter now, regretting his choice of words.

Please god, let me be wrong, he thought.

"Sorry." He shook it off. "It's not. I'll explain later, I promise."

He gave her the best smile he could forge and kissed her lightly on her rain-soaked forehead.

"So, what have we got?"

.   .   .

WHAT THEY HAD COULD ONLY BE DESCRIBED as medieval. Like something from the darkest pages of the bible, or the most horrific corners of history. Contrasted against the dull blue grey of the rock face were the bodies of two young people. Each suspended, roughly fifteen foot off of the ground, each hung from meat hooks, connected into some of the climbing bolts that had been drilled into the cliff. Each with their face covered by a mask in the shape of a pig. If he had not been in Ainsley's company, then the look on Graham's face would have been one of awe instead of disgust.

AINSLEY REACHED down with her hand to find his fingers. She found them, and he squeezed and hung on for dear life. She could hear his breathing, getting faster, gathering pace, and matching the beads of sweat forming on his forehead. His face was stony though, cold, and at that moment she wished she could read his mind.

"Our killer thinks he is something of an artist," he said, after a long moment of silence.

THERE'S *that fucking coincidence again.*

"A what?" Ainsley replied.

One of the SOCO techs pushed past Graham, muttering something under his breath as he struggled along with arms full of heavy camera equipment. Graham returned his gaze to the rock.

"An artist. He's upping the ante with each kill. Sophie was rushed, a bit of a botch job, but he still left her in public view. Our killer laid Jessica out carefully, almost reputably. But this..." He motioned back and forth to the pair of corpses hanging before him. "This is really quite something."

"Have you lost the fucking plot?" Ainsley snapped.

Graham ignored her and squinted to read something pinned to one of the victims.

"Becky?" he said.

"What?"

"The name tag stabbed through her left breast. It says Becky on it. Should make identification a tad easier, I suppose. Do we have an ID for the other one yet?"

"Graham, maybe now is not the time."

Again, he ignored her, and instead called out to another member of the SOCO team.

"Any chance of us getting them down, or getting those stupid fucking masks off at least?"

As the first mask was removed, Graham realised he recognised the girl as the barista from the café back in the city. He had seen her alive only a few days ago.

Jesus fuck, he thought, closing his eyes and rubbing his head. *Now that's three.*

"And the other."

Everyone there recoiled in horror as the second mask came away from the victim's face. Everyone, that was, besides Graham. He knew. Deep inside, he knew from the moment he woke up on that hard wooden floor.

OH, no. Lewis.

34

THE HOUSE LOOKED MUCH different in the dark. However, it wasn't that 'wave a hand in front of your face' dark. The headlamps of the passing cars and non-stop glare from the streetlights saw to that. But it was dark enough for someone to slip into a corner and be alone with their thoughts and regrets. It was as if it provided you with your own personal all-surrounding cocoon. And for Graham, that was just what he needed.

He had only been sitting there for perhaps an hour or two, but the debilitating effects of half a bottle of cheap corner shop whisky were beginning to take effect. Graham sobbed into his knees while one hand gripped the smooth glass on the neck of the bottle. His other lay flat on the floor, the tips of its fingers bloodied, as he had been clawing at the wood of the living room floor.

"Lewis... Lewis, I am so sorry mate," he said as he knocked back a mouthful of the whisky.

He wiped the snot from his lip, catching it just as it went to enter the corner of his trembling mouth.

"I know it's my fault. I should have told you; I should have confided in you."

Graham struggled to his feet and took another large gulp from the bottle, most of which made its way down his front and onto the floor. He looked to the ceiling light as he swayed back and forth on intoxicated legs. He looked at the light and spoke to it as if it were Lewis himself.

"Do you want to know what the worst thing is? I could tell Elena what I think... no, what I *know* about *him*. But she would never fucking believe me. She *has* to believe me. She has to stay away."

Graham paced the room. He moved up and down it like an inebriated predatory animal. Liquid sloshed from the bottle as he swung it wide back and forth, not once taking his gaze from the light fitting above his head. He spoke faster now, his voice almost frantic.

"He must have known I was on to him. Maybe he knew I was following him. Jesus, maybe he was following me, following us, Lew."

Graham's gaze turned to the appearance of yet another set of car headlights in his living room window. These seemed to linger somewhat, long enough, he thought, for the bars of light that came streaming through the gap in the curtains to pick up on the clouds of dust that danced majestically across the room, and served as a reminder of just how much he had let his housekeeping slip as of late.

"Just some scumbags from down the road, I reckon," he said, pulling his gaze back to the 'Lewis' light. "What was I saying? Yeah... he must have been on to me..."

Thump, thump, thump.

The banging on the door broke Graham's train of

thought once more and he spun on his heels, scowling towards the front of the house.

"Bugger off. I'm busy," he called out, dropping the bottle on top of one of his bare feet as he completed the turn.

Yelling out in frustration, he kicked the bottle hard into the skirting board, which only helped to further the pain in his foot. The remaining booze bled onto the wooden floor, and he sank to his knees to suck as much of it up as he could before it soaked into the wood. If he was honest, it didn't taste all that different to when it had been fresh from the bottle, and with no one to witness it, he felt no shame in it at all.

Thump, thump, thump.

"Piss off, I said. Are you deaf or just fucking stupid?"

"THANKS AGAIN FOR THE LIFT, AINSLEY," Elena said as she slid into the passenger's seat of the Vauxhall Astra and closed the door.

The car was immaculate, just like the driver, and the smell of citrus fruit and vanilla from the little tree hanging in the mirror was a welcome lift after the past few days. She thrust her sodden umbrella into the footwell and clipped her seat belt on, throwing her chauffeur a warm, heartfelt smile as she did.

"Don't be silly," Ainsley replied, rubbing Elena's leg with warm affection. "After the way he was, I think it best if we go and see him together."

"The way he was?"

Ainsley sighed deeply as she turned the car's engine over. It roared into life, and she rubbed her brow vigorously as she pulled them into the queue of traffic.

"It was like he was entranced. He was an emotionless

robot. It was like he was on autopilot, going through the motions. And then he was gone."

"Maybe it's just his way of coping."

"You know him better than I do, and even I know his way of coping is to be found at the bottom of a bottle."

Elena looked out of the passenger window. She bit her lip to stem her cries, the building anger, even going as far as to quickly wipe a stray tear with the sleeve of her hoodie, hoping that Ainsley would not see. But it was no good. In better judgement though, Ainsley gave her the time to think, not wanting to pry, not wanting to push the fragile girl any further.

"He was doing so well," Elena finally managed a short while later from beneath a choked sob.

"And he will again dear, hopefully."

Elena's phone vibrated loudly in her hand. Rolling her eyes, she turned the device over to look at it.

Incoming call – Jackson

3 Missed Calls

2 New Messages

She threw it into the footwell alongside the umbrella while muttering something under her breath. Ainsley clearly picked up on the sentiment and chuckled.

"How are things with you two?"

"It's just *me* until he apologises in a way that isn't piss-weak."

THE CAR ROUNDED the last corner and on to the street which housed Graham's home. The building sat in total darkness, and Ainsley pulled the car onto the kerb outside, letting the engine idle as the headlights probed the windows for any sign of life. The two women exited the car together, silently, and made their way up the concrete path to the front door. Ainsley took Elena's hand in her own and squeezed it with an almost maternal love, offering her what smile she could through the gloom of the evening's weather. Without a word, Elena extended her arm and knocked.

Greeted by an all-too-familiar sight as the door opened, Elena pushed past the shell of her father, and moved to turn on the living room lights, almost intuitively. She passed a spilled bottle on her way, picked it up without as much as a second thought, and placed it on the table to her left.

He went to speak, to attempt to explain about this, about their situation, and she did the same. But before either could mutter as much as a syllable, Ainsley was between them, her face as dark as the clouds outside, eyes sharp, with lips pursed into a tight grimace. Seeing the pain behind his eyes, however, her face softened.

"You are not alone in this Grah—" she went to say.

"Jackson," he blurted out, swaying violently to one side, knocking a vase flying from the side table. "It was Jackson."

"What was Jackson?" Elena demanded.

She pushed herself so close to him she could taste the whisky on his breath, almost convinced she could set it alight with a single match.

"What the hell are you on about?"

He flailed his arms around in every direction as tears burned his eyes and streamed down his face. He was communicating the best he could, considering his inebriated state.

"This... All of this," he pleaded. "Lewis, fucking all of it. It's *him*, Elena."

Elena stopped dead as the colour ran from her face and the air in the room turned icy cold. Her hands trembled.

Ainsley searched each of their faces in turn, not knowing what to say or do. There was a long, uncomfortable silence.

Elena finally stepped forward. Her green eyes met with the pleading blue of her father's as she raised her right hand and struck him flat on his left cheek. Her palm throbbed and burned, as did the tears in her eyes.

"We came here to help you, to offer you some comfort, and this is what you give."

"Elen—"

"Stop," she barked, jabbing an extended finger at the empty bottle on the table behind them. "No more. You pushed mum away by knocking that shit back, and now it seems like you want to do the same to me, the same to Ainsley, for fuck's sake, and god knows she doesn't need your shit. I know you're hurting for Lewis, but you're sick to bring Jackson into this. The only person to blame is you. You're pathetic."

He reached for her, but she pulled away and backtracked to the front door.

"Ainsley, I can't do this, I'm sorry."

Before either Graham or Ainsley could say a word, the door slammed shut, and the two of them were left standing in the living room, with the scent of stale alcohol and heavy emotion hanging in the air. Ainsley closed her eyes and breathed deeply, taking Graham's hand in hers.

"I think we should talk," she said softly. "I'll pop the kettle on."

35

IT WAS ALL A BLUR, how he got there. An intense and incomprehensible blur of emotion, regrets and intoxicated thoughts. The events of the past few days had brought it all to the surface. Wounds both new and historic were split wide open, they festered, leaching into every crevice of his existence, and were taking centre stage in the thundering and bustling concert that was his mind. To Graham, the 'how' was insignificant, perhaps even somewhat trivial. But the fact that he was now sitting at his desk, facing an empty chair, was crushing.

The Bull Pen was more often than not at the unsociable side of rowdy. But that morning the noise that was normally almost deafening, was crippling. Together with the aroma of strong coffee and the lingering bouquet of body odour and cheap aftershave, Graham struggled to think, to function. Managing nothing more than a hollow grin, that itself was nothing more than a front, he had got through the tide of greetings and condolences with some manner of grace. However, it was the inevitable, and quite possibly uncomfortable, conversation he was bound to have with Detective Chief Inspector Morgan at some point that morning that kept him from diving headfirst through the second-storey window, and into a comfy, permanent bed on the concrete below.

I have to be on this case, he kept telling himself, over and over, repeating it as though it were a mantra. *For Lewis. For Elena. For my own sanity.*

He did his best to wade through the pre-briefing paperwork that had been left for him. The briefing itself was not scheduled to start for another twenty minutes, so at least he had some time to get his head around some of the details. The major facts were clear, he had seen them for himself, firsthand at the quarry, but there was much he did not know. The girl's full identity, for example, or the contents of the pathologist's report, that was sitting to the left of his desk, and signed off in Ainsley's neat hand.

Ainsley, he thought, brushing his fingers gently over the file.

Their conversation the night before had not gone as badly as he had expected. Although he found out why she had left her husband some years back; he *also* had a problem with alcohol, which made Graham feel like more of a fool. For reasons unknown to them both, she was willing to stick around and help him through it all. He was mad about her before, infatuated, but now the draw he felt towards her had intensified tenfold. She could be his light at the end of the tunnel, and he was damned if he was going to do anything now to extinguish it.

. . .

THE COFFEE, although hardly what you could call premium, got the job done. It warmed him from the inside out, and the rush of caffeine helped the pages to pass with greater frequency and clarity. From the corner of one of his eyes, Graham noticed Andrews moving with quite some considerable pace, which was surprising considering his stout stature, across the office and towards DCI Morgan with a fist full of papers. Morgan, never the man to interrupt, especially as he was preparing to brief the team, snatched the papers from Andrews and gave them the once over with a scowl. His face dropped. Morgan raised his head, ever so slowly, and gazed in Graham's direction, giving him a cold, fixed stare. Graham's heart leapt into his throat and his skin began to crawl.

What the fuck is on that paper? he wondered.

Morgan jammed a chubby finger in his direction and motioned for Graham to follow him, which he did without thought. The sound of Morgan's office door slamming behind them cut through the tension and drowned out the noise from beyond its flaking frame. Silence. A few moments of an uneasy silence, in which both DCI Morgan and Andrews eyed Graham up and down in tense contemplation. After a while, though, Morgan cleared his throat.

"Graham, what did you say happened to your mobile phone?"

"Just that it had vanished. Must have fallen out of my pocket somewhere, I guess. Why do you ask?"

Morgan looked down at the papers in his hand and then shot an uneasy look to Andrews, who was standing off to one side. Graham shuffled on the spot, and beneath his shirt collar he had already started to sweat. He did not like where this was going.

"As with all of our victims thus far, none of Lewis' personal possessions were recovered from the crime scene. Including his mobile phone."

Morgan pulled out his desk chair and sat down, folding his hands on top of the bundle of papers.

"Sir?"

"We still haven't traced DS Reed's phone, but we do have the last few messages to and from it thanks to his service provider."

Morgan handed Graham the papers, which turned out to be a transcript of the last texts pulled from Lewis' phone. He fought back the urge to well up as he fingered through the pages.

"Is that... a grid reference?" Graham asked after a while, pointing to one of the sheets that was now heavily crumpled.

"Aye," Andrews said. "To a remote spot up in the Beacons."

"It's an empty cottage," Morgan interjected. "Land registry has it being disused for some time now, a good spot for a killer to do their work, wouldn't you agree? Lewis' car has yet to be found as well, and I'll bet my year's salary we'll find it up there."

"Whoever sent these messages lured him up there," Andrews said.

"We're assembling a team as we speak to go and look," Morgan said. "But the thing is... the thing is, Graham... These messages were sent from *your* phone."

The room fell silent once again. Graham's knees weakened, and he struggled to keep his balance.

"In light of this," Morgan continued before Graham could get a word in, "I have placed you on indefinite leave, pending further investigation."

"Sir, I—"

"I don't want to hear it, Walker," he snapped. "I find it unlikely that our killer just happened across your phone. I don't take you for a monster, but until this is all cleared up, or you start talking, I do not want you anywhere near this case. Am I clear?"

"I can help," Graham pleaded.

"Jesus Christ, man. You can barely help yourself. You look like a tramp and smell like a pub I would never want to go to. Do us all a favour and go home, don't make a scene."

Graham lowered his head, defeated.

"Steve..." he said from beneath a choked sob.

Morgan lowered his voice. He almost sounded compassionate. "Not another word, Graham, I have something else to tell you. I've pushed the coroner to release Lewis' body to his family as soon as practical. They need to be allowed to grieve for him properly, as do we."

"How soon?"

Morgan sighed. "Today, Graham."

Graham raised his head. Tears were forming in his blue, shattered eyes. They burned, and he struggled to see. Andrews placed a large, friendly hand on his shoulder and squeezed. Graham looked Morgan in the eye, but said nothing. He just nodded.

"You are going to have to keep your distance, Gray. His parents are having him buried at the end of the week. I think it's in all of our best interests that you are not there, not unless we can resolve this mess beforehand."

GRAHAM SAID NOTHING. But inside, he managed to compose himself. He wanted to maintain some of his self-respect amongst his peers. So, he picked himself up, stood straight, and placed the papers back on Morgan's desk neatly. He would leave quietly; he would not make a scene. But he would get his facts straight. He would get the evidence he needed. And then he would be back.

36

"COME TO THINK OF IT, maybe she should join you, after all," Jackson said aloud as he fingered through the open box of trophies sitting beside the hole in the floor. "Would you believe that she's forgiven me already, no questions asked?"

He picked up a small, black phone with a grey cover. One of the newest to his collection. Feeling almost giddy, he put it to his face and inhaled. The scent sent a shiver down his spine, and he let out a small, choked laugh.

"You were nothing more than an opportunity. A sorbet, of sorts, if you will. A chance to cleanse my palate. The whole experience was most enjoyable, if a little unexpected, I must say."

Jackson's skin broke out in gooseflesh as he spoke, and he had to close his eyes to calm his breathing.

"She has even invited me to *your* funeral, detective. Oh, what fun *that* will be. They're all too stupid to see what's really in front of them, you see. Blinded by love. That's not a mistake that I'll make as well."

He looked at another of the phones in the small, wooden box. This one, the one with a broken screen, brought light into his otherwise stony expression. He traced the edges of the fractured glass with his finger, cutting its tip on a stray shard. He lifted the finger and watched as the crimson liquid seeped from beneath his pale flesh and dripped down past each knuckle. The sight of it, and the metallic taste when it contacted his tongue, made him flush, and brought life into his groin.

"It feels like an empty victory if I'm quite honest, Mr Walker," he said, rubbing his tongue on his teeth and now talking to the *damaged* device. "You see, regardless of my inconsistencies, and the fact that I just up and leave when I please without explanation, all it takes to get her back onside is a wink, some kind words, and the drop of one's trousers. On closer inspection, she is actually rather pathetic, Mr Walker, a little like yourself. It's true what they say, after all. The apple doesn't fall far from the tree."

His dry chuckle erupted into a fit of hysteric laughter as he threw the phone back into the box.

"Like a cat with a mouse, I suppose I'm just getting bored. It appears as though I have misjudged her. I am only human, after all."

He stood and admired his naked form in the full-length mirror. The soft light of the late morning sun filtered through the window blinds and cast shadows across his toned physique. Allowing himself a subtle grin of satisfaction, he turned and made his way towards the bathroom.

"Perhaps it is time to leave her head on someone's doorstep."

.   .   .

IT HAD BEEN many years since the old cottage had seen so much life between its walls. In decades past, the masterfully built stone building stood proud in the mountainous valley. It had welcomed visitors, friends, and family alike, through its green painted oak front door, and into a home warmed by love and a roaring fire. It had been a pleasing respite from the cold and winds that ripped through the valley, between the peaks and the trees, and around the eaves of the cottage itself. A home. A proper home. Where memories were created, and dreams were nurtured. A far cry from what it had become.

The kitchen, handcrafted and beautiful, with its polished slate floor, once the heart of the family home, stood in ruin. A gaping hole in the roof, some two metres across, had opened it to the elements and allowed nature to restate its claim from the top down. The degradation and rot started here and worked its way to all four corners of the building. The investigatory team, consisting of a number of detectives and SOCO officers, stood around the remains of the kitchen table, and peered up through the roof to the heavens above.

"You can smell the bleach in the air," Detective Chief Inspector Morgan said.

"I know," Andrews replied, cupping a gloved hand to his mouth. "I can fucking taste it."

Morgan crouched down to examine the floor. Scuff marks, chips of missing slate; were they from years past, or perhaps from a more recent visitor? He drew something in the dirt with his finger. He stared at it in silence for a long moment, and scrutinised it, and then just brushed it away.

"Ainsley," he called out, getting to his feet.

As normal, the entire SOCO team was clad head to toe in white paper suits, masks and all. Between that, and the intense light provided by their floodlights, which seemed to only diminish visibility in the room by highlighting the amount of dust in the air, there was no way in hell he was going to recognise her by sight alone.

A pale figure appeared from beyond the doorway to his left, carrying a clipboard under its arm. It walked with prowess and confidence towards Morgan with a raised hand.

"Sir," Ainsley replied, muffled from behind her mask.

"Does your team have anything yet?"

She pulled back the hood of her paper suit, revealing a brow sodden with sweat, with hair to match. Her eyes, normally so calm and reflective, burned with a ferocious determination, and she pulled her mask down to speak.

"The car out front is Lewis', like we thought. No obvious signs of forced entry or stains that could be perceived as blood. We've pulled fibres, hairs, most likely his own, but we'll run them anyway. If I'm honest, it looks like what we imagined. He drove here under his own power. But in here..." she motioned to the room that they were all standing in, "Jesus, the amount of blood the UVs have picked up on is insane. If I was a betting woman, I would say that this room, this kitchen, this is our kill site."

A GENTLE NOD in her direction showed his agreement. Although a forensic pathologist by trade, because of her keen eye and incredible work ethic, Morgan had insisted that she head up the SOCO team on this investigation. There could be no room for error today, not when it concerned one of their own, and Morgan trusted her judgement more than anyone else's.

· · ·

THIS USED TO BE A HOME, she thought.

Ainsley shifted nervously on the spot as she thought back to another house. *Graham's* house. Where he was now, rattling around and probably going mad. She thought he should have been there with them, working the case, working to bring Lewis' killer to justice. For all of his faults, and there were many, nobody could argue that he wasn't a bloody fine copper.

"...and it's been scrubbed clean, as I'm sure your nose has already told you."

She consulted her clipboard briefly before continuing. Ainsley was never comfortable reporting to the brass, especially when delivering bad news, and her body language showed it.

"So far, nothing of use has been discovered. He, or they, wanted us to find this place, so I imagine anything we do find could have possibly been staged."

"So, they're fucking toying with us?" Morgan replied gruffly.

"Sure looks that way."

"Bollocks," he replied, shoving a stick of chewing gum into his down-turned mouth. "I want a full report on my desk by day's end, am I clear? I can't waste any more time standing here in this shit hole. I have a meeting with the detective chief superintendent to prepare for. She wants a progress report. So, if you can give me anything, I would really appreciate it. Andrews, you're with me."

Before she could reply to the DCI, he spun on his heels and headed for the door. She shared an uncomfortable look with Andrews before he, too, made for the exit.

No worries lads, she thought as she refitted her mask and clicked her pen open. *Leave it to me.*

· · ·

GRAHAM WAS fast asleep by the time Ainsley returned to his house that night and slid into bed next to him. The house was immaculate, she noted on her way upstairs, so at least he had kept himself busy. But how long was that going to last? She could not smell any alcohol on him either when she snuggled in tight to him, which was a welcome bonus that she had not been expecting.

She had been hoping to get back to him much earlier, to talk about Lewis' funeral, which was planned to take place in the local church the following morning. She knew he was crushed at not being able to be there, but she had decided to go anyway, to represent them both.

THE AROMA of freshly brewed coffee and the unmistakable aroma of bacon and eggs woke Ainsley in the morning. A pleasant surprise in itself, but made all the more pleasing by the bright eyes and toothy smile of the man who had leaned over and kissed her good morning.

"Long day?" he asked as he placed the breakfast tray down at the foot of bed and poured them both a drink.

She sat and brushed the stray, tangled mess of hair from her face. Graham offered her a mug of the steaming, sweet brown liquid, which she accepted and drank with eagerness.

"Thank you," she began, gently removing the cup from her lips. "Yeah, you could say that. And all for nothing it seems."

"Oh, how so?"

"It was a setup. The whole thing."

Graham lifted a tentative eyebrow and took a seat on the end of the bed, motioning for her to continue.

"Gray...Gray, I think you're right about the whole thing, well, most of it at least."

"Most of it?"

"I still cannot fathom Jackson having any involvement."

He rolled his eyes and used the coffee mug to try and hide his agitation.

"But," she continued, ignoring the look on his face, "whoever had access to your phone definitely lured Lewis there under some pretence or another. We found his car. It wasn't left there by accident, though. He cleaned it. The whole scene was immaculate, in fact, and we didn't find much really. That is, apart from confirming that it was more than likely the kill site. Gray, you should have seen what the UV picked up."

"Jesus Christ. So, we were always meant to find the cottage?"

"Yeah. I mean, it's sure looking that way."

"It's all just a bloody game," he said from behind gritted teeth.

"Hey, you," Ainsley said as she took one of his clenched fists into her hands. "We don't need to talk about this today. Let's eat some breakfast, it smells great."

They both attacked the large breakfast spread with good appetite, with Graham helping himself to a second round of bacon sandwiches after what had been an already colossal first helping. They spoke of the weather, and of something that Graham had seen on the previous evening's news, but deep down each knew of the inevitable words that were due from Ainsley's mouth.

"Right then, thank you for that, but I had better get going."

"What time does it start?" he asked, trying his hardest to hold back any glimpse of the torment he felt. She could, however, read him like a book.

Ainsley leaned across and rubbed the tops of his hands

with her gentle fingers. She looked deep into the blue pools of his eyes, which, she noted, had filled, and kissed him lightly on the forehead.

"Quarter past twelve," she started as she pulled herself from him. "Look, don't you worry, it's just some formal faff. He... Lewis, I mean, knows you are thinking of him. I bet he knows you haven't stopped thinking of him."

"I know. It's just some formal faff that I would have liked to be a part of. To be honest, if he knew I was blubbering like this he would be taking the piss. But still..."

He trailed off and stared out of the window into the little garden beyond in an attempt to hide any further tears from Ainsley. But it didn't work.

"I'll come back here after. I'll make us a nice dinner. How does that sound?"

He offered only a nod and a weak smile as she rose from her perch. She looked radiant, that much he knew. The black dress she wore hugged her body in all the right places; and she was wearing her hair up, which he thought was a nice change, as he could see her face for the true beauty that it was. She had not even left the house yet, but he already missed her greatly.

"I'll see you later," she said, turning for the door.

He grabbed her hand and stood to kiss her, pulling her into his chest. Caught rather off guard, she let out a little giggle as their lips parted.

"I can't wait."

37

OCTOBER 1ST 2018, 12:10

CLOUDS GATHERED above at the same pace as the people on each side of the pavement. Their dark suits, dresses and shoes perfectly mirrored the contrast of the gloom overhead. The first drops of unexpected rain dabbled the surface of the concrete as the procession rounded the corner, and made its way solemnly towards the church.

The funeral director, who preceded the wagon of death, walked slowly, his footsteps in time with the pounding of the rain upon the concrete. His face remained frozen, unmoving, during his traverse of the long road. Whether it was due to a strong sense of professional pride, or some deep personal battle within himself, his expression perfectly captured the day's mood, and was found to be mirrored on the faces of each of the people who came to line the streets that day.

As the procession came to a halt outside the grand oak doors of the church, the view, as it was for this spectator, was masked by the ocean of black and grey that was the attending mourners. He knew what was happening though. He had witnessed it, and even been a part of it many times before. The car behind the hearse would spew forth the weeping family of the deceased, who would lead the congregation inside behind the box that housed the vessel that had once been their son. He wondered who would take his place carrying Lewis inside. Andrews? Or Morgan, perhaps.

Surely not, he thought, as he brushed rain from his brow. *What about Jackson?*

He was repulsed at the thought, but knew full well that the pool of potential candidates for the role was shallow at best. Lewis had been well liked by the people that knew him, but he had made a conscious effort in life to keep that circle small. So, who was left? He tried to push the thought from his mind and hunker down in position for a better view.

GRAHAM'S CURRENT VANTAGE POINT, a well-placed gap between two towering ash trees at the end of a field that faced the church, provided little shelter from the weather. He had been there now for perhaps only twenty minutes, but he was already soaked to the bone and shivering.

Slowly, the crowd filtered inside, and for the first time, Graham could fully appreciate the towering spectacle that stood before him. A gothic architectural masterpiece that dominated the local skyline, embossed with all manner of imagery including gargoyles, angels and sheets of jaw-dropping stained glass. He was not a religious man, not by any stretch, but standing there beneath the church as the first hymns swelled from the service within, he felt something.

It started as an uneasy sensation that climbed the length

of his spine, making the hairs on the back of his neck stand on end. And it culminated in a rush of adrenalin that brought with it memories. Memories of Lewis – the good and the bad. It made him smile, it made him cry. Most of all, however, it filled him with an immense sense of pride to have known and worked alongside such an incredible man. A man he was proud to have called his friend.

TIME PASSED SLOWLY out in the cold. To warm his body, and to prepare for the next stage of the day, Graham made his way quietly to the rear of the church. His sodden and dishevelled appearance definitely raised a few eyebrows from passersby as he crossed the road. But he ignored them.

Let them stare, he thought.

Graham stood astride the hole that had been dug for his friend, and he enjoyed the earthy smell from the damp, loose earth as it entered his airways. He had a few minutes at best, he thought, standing there between the gravestones and rotting flowers, as the hymns gave way to what he recognised as Lewis' favourite song. Even in death, Graham thought his choice in music was terrible, and the thought of it brought a little light into his face.

He raised his head in the church's direction, threw it back, and allowed himself a hearty laugh. *Honestly, Lew? Lionel fucking Richie?*

Thankfully, the rain had eased somewhat by the time the funeral procession had gathered around Lewis' final resting place. Graham had a much better view this time round, perched on the bottom step of an adjacent mausoleum that shadowed his form from view. It was from here that he saw it.

· · ·

AFTER SOME MORE TALKING, which Graham figured to be just some religious mumbo-jumbo, and a lot more crying, Lewis' coffin was finally lowered into the ground. He spied Ainsley, looking as beautiful as she had early that morning, making small talk with Andrews and Morgan as the crowd dispersed. But it was the person who stood beyond them that really caught his eye. Elena. Not too unusual. She had known Lewis well, but she was *not* alone. *He*, Jackson, had one arm around her waist and carried her bag in his other hand. He shook hands with Andrews, Morgan, and all the other police officers there, radiating a confidence that no man, especially not him, should have had. But it was not his attendance, or the smugness, that set Graham off.

It all happened in the blink of an eye. Jackson leaned in to condole with Lewis' mother, but before he had even a chance to speak, Graham was between them. He had not even realised that he had stood up, let alone crossed the twenty-five metres or so of graveyard, to get there.

"Back off, you poisonous little prick," Graham spat as if it were venom, shoving Jackson back with the flat of his hand.

"Dad."

"Walker, what the hell are you doing here?" Morgan demanded.

The crowd parted around them as if they were on fire. Gasps could be heard all around, and above it all, Lewis' mother cried hysterically. Graham and Jackson's eyes met in a tense battle of nerve, neither man taking his gaze from the other.

"This *is* our killer," Graham said as he jammed a finger towards Jackson, who remained silent and unmoved. "Sophie, Jessica and now Becky and Lewis as well, on top of Christ knows how many more."

Elena tried, from beyond tear-filled eyes, to pull her father back, but it was no use.

"Dad, are you insane?" she cried.

"Walker, what the hell is this? What do you *think* you're doing?" Morgan added.

"Stay out of this, Steve."

"You're the psycho, Dad, you need help," Elena said.

Ainsley reached out with a loving hand and pulled her back, trying to calm her and stop her from clawing at Graham's back.

It was at that moment that a tiny smile broke on Jackson's face, and he leaned forward to finally speak, being careful that only Graham could hear.

"She's right, and you fucking know it," he whispered.

WITHOUT HESITATION OR SECOND THOUGHT, Graham brought his right fist into flat contact with Jackson's cheek, sending him backwards and onto the floor. What followed went past in a blur.

THERE WERE ONLY two things that Graham could remember before being manhandled into the back of a police car. The screams: Elena's screams, Ainsley's perhaps, and most definitely Lewis' mother's. And *his* face: the smile that crossed his muddied and bleeding face through the crowd as Graham was being dragged away. It followed him. And it was haunting.

38

THE FAINT SQUEAK that was created by the contact of shoes and the aged, grey linoleum, reverberated off the walls as she took each careful, calculated step. The air down there was cold and stale. The stench of cheap industrial cleaners clung to the inside of her nose and brought tears to her eyes. This was not her first time down here, and the sounds and smells brought the memories rushing back. She had been here many times as a child. She had been shown around and allowed to explore every nook and cranny, just so long as the cells had been empty. But she had never been here to visit a prisoner. There would be no hide and seek this time around, no chocolate-covered face and giggles of glee. This was a first, and it made her palms sweat.

A young, uniformed officer stood with his arms crossed and a face like stone as Elena approached the door of cell four with DCI Morgan in tow. The officer quickly stood to attention as soon as he spied Morgan, and let out a whimpering "sir", before turning to unlock the way.

The heavy steel door, which looked as though it had seen several slap-dash coats of grey paint over the years, moaned against its hinges as the young man battled to pull it fully open. It crashed against the exposed concrete block wall with a heavy thud that echoed down the hall, and flakes of the old paint fluttered to the ground like post-apocalyptic snowflakes caught in a breeze. Morgan motioned her inside, but she stood there considering for a long moment. After some time had passed in silence, she lifted her head, drew in a deep breath, and crossed the threshold.

SHE FOUND his face in the gloom. Muddied and bruised from the day's earlier events, but not broken or defeated, as she had expected. Graham held his head high, despite his surroundings, and met Elena's gaze. What little light penetrated the drab space through the small, single window found its way to him and illuminated his face. His blue eyes were alive with fire and shone with an intensity that she had not seen for some time, and, if she was honest, it caught her rather off guard.

"Dad," she said quietly to break the silence.

Graham did not answer for a long time. Elena's voice hung in the air, and only the sound of his deep and controlled breathing cut through the tension. His presence made her uneasy, and she found herself standing, staring at the bare concrete floor, clutching one arm at the elbow like a schoolgirl waiting for a good telling off. Relaxing his pose, he opened his palms to her, and eventually spoke.

"Come in, kid. We should talk."

· · ·

A FEW MILES ACROSS TOWN, basking in the autumn sun that had escaped from between the day's earlier darkness, Jackson made his way down the high street with a spring in his step. He was no longer clad in the solemn, unflattering funeral suit of the morning. Instead, he had opted for a striking red and green flannel shirt matched to smart black, skinny jeans, over which he wore an expensive crimson hiking jacket embroidered with the logo of a popular outdoor clothing brand.

A large smile embossed his freshly shaven face. And for a man who had attended a funeral, and been punched square in the face earlier that day, his mood was rather upbeat. Not even the gawks and comments from passersby, concerning the fat lip and black eye that now adorned his otherwise classically attractive face, could dampen his spirits. He even entertained some of them with a small wave and a wink.

Jackson dropped into his favourite little café on the way past. They were short staffed, and the queue was long. But regardless, the coffee was just as good as it had been before. Even if the view was not. He thought it funny, even somewhat ironic, that considering how much the owners of the café had missed Becky sorely (according to their social media posts at least) that a "help wanted" sign was already up in the window, front, and centre. Jackson shook his head and laughed.

It seems when all is said and done, we are all replaceable, he thought.

It was love that fuelled his elated mood that afternoon. Not a love for a person or thing, that would be far too pedestrian, but a love for victory. It was victory over an adversary, even one that he felt to be at times a little pathetic, that awarded him this feeling of power that burned deep within him. He looked around the high street to the people who surrounded him, going about their business completely unaware of what he was capable of or what he had done. They were textbook examples of the mundane, he thought, and next to them he was godly.

Victory, however, came at a price. And for Jackson Page, that price was named Pandora, and a certain box in her possession. A box that, when opened with greater regularity, became harder and harder to close. It had only been days since his last, but already he was hungry and on the prowl. He was not necessarily expecting to find anyone worthy on this busy Cardiff afternoon, but he soon spied a potential candidate through the window of a travel agent that sent chills down his spine, and heat into his groin.

He dropped his empty coffee cup into a nearby bin and allowed himself a small grin.

A holiday would be nice, he thought.

"DAD, you sound barking mad, can't you see that?" Elena said as she paced the tiny space for the hundredth time.

"It's the truth, kid. Please, you have to believe me. I was drugged."

"Is that something we can prove?" she asked, directing the question to DCI Morgan, who stood leaning against the door frame with his arms crossed, listening to their conversation intently.

"Maybe. But we would have to have some idea what we were looking for."

"The same shit he has been pumping into these girls," Graham barked.

"You know full well—"

"That nothing came up on their bloods, I know."

Morgan raised a palm and an eyebrow in Graham's direction, his face somewhat apologetic. Graham read the sentiment and sank his head into his hands.

"Jesus, Steve, this is madness."

"Without evidence or just cause, I cannot authorise..."

"Just cause?" he said, cutting across his DCI frantically. "Now you must be pulling my leg. When are the cameras coming in, guys? Graham Walker, you have been punked."

"This is not a joke, Graham."

"And I'm not fucking laughing, Steven."

The two men glared at each other, burning figurative holes through each other's skulls. Silence re-entered the space, followed by a wave of unwaning tension. The only sounds were the heavy breaths of each of the unmoving alpha males, who were locked in a seemingly unending staring contest.

"You're letting him go, right?" Elena said eventually to cut through the atmosphere. "He isn't being charged with anything?"

Sighing, the situation clearly weighing heavily on him, DCI Morgan turned to her, and his face softened.

"Yeah, he's free to go. But Graham," he said, turning to face him, "there's something I need to ask you, and I'll only ask you this once."

"Am I under caution?" he fired back sarcastically.

"You know full well you are not. Not yet, at least. But if you do have anything to say, now would be the time."

Morgan finally entered the cell and made his way to the tiny window at the end. He gazed out of it, through the rusted iron bars, and spied the lowering sun just as it began its descent towards the horizon. He took a deep breath and clasped his hands behind his back.

"Graham, where were you the night Lewis died?"

The colour drained from Graham's face almost immediately, and he let out a small, nervous laugh. He used the palms of his hands to rub at his face frantically before standing up, with his face hard and blue eyes piercing and wild.

"Looks like I might need a solicitor then," he said matter-of-factly as he headed for the door.

Without turning from the window, Morgan called out, a harsh chill in his voice, "I wouldn't go too far, Graham, if I were you."

THE ENGINE of Graham's Jeep droned in the background as he and Elena walked down the two flights of concrete steps into the car park. Ainsley was behind its wheel and greeted them each with a nervous wave.

The clouds, which had earlier parted to reveal stunning blue skies, had returned. And the bitter wind that accompanied them fluttered the bottom of Elena's funeral dress, and brought her skin to gooseflesh. Graham motioned for her to embrace him, but to say that she was hesitant would be an understatement.

He took a confident step forward and pulled his daughter into his breast. She struggled at first, but as the warmth he provided comforted her, and his scent brought her love for him to the forefront, she committed fully to the embrace and cried hysterically.

"Dad, I don't know what to believe."

"Use your head, kid." He lifted her chin with one muddied finger and brushed the hair from her eyes so that he could see her face fully. "Always follow your heart. But *never* forget to use your head. And on that note, I need you to do something for me."

"And what's that?" she said, sniffling.

Graham sighed. "Stay away from that boy. I mean it, Elena. He's dangerous."

As the car drove away and the rain fell, a nearby bush parted. A smiling figure, clutching a handful of sun-draped holiday brochures, stepped forward onto the tarmac. He wiped the rain from his forehead and scoffed.

"We cannot be having that now, can we?"

39

OCTOBER 2ND 2018, 11:45

"A HOLIDAY? That's your big surprise?" Elena said.

"You don't think it's a good idea?"

"No, no, it's great but... the timing..."

"Lewis?"

"Yeah, that, but my dad too."

Jackson scoffed and stole a glance in the rear-view mirror to see his face. The bruising around his eye had yellowed, and the swelling around his lip had gone down, but the split remained.

"I'm sure even *he* could see why it would be a good idea," he said, with a hint of venom on his tongue. "A bit of sun will do you... will do *us* some good. Are you coming?"

Elena looked left, and then right, down the street. She could still hear her dad's voice in her ears. His rantings. His warnings. But all it had done was confuse matters for her further.

"I...I mean, do I need to?"

"I would much prefer your company when going to book *us* a holiday, yes. But I would never force you. You are your own woman, after all."

What do I do? she thought.

As Jackson pulled the car into a parking space and switched the engine off, light appeared across his face. He leaned across and took Elena's hand, rather forcefully, as she initially resisted, and kissed her on the cheek, smiling.

"We're here," he said with some air of glee. "You couldn't grab the brochures out of the glove box as you get out, could you? I can't wait to show you my plans."

Taken aback and confused, as if the past few days had been nothing more than a terrible dream, Elena complied, giving him a nod and an uneasy smile as she slid from the black leather seat and into the brisk wind of the day.

"You'll be stoked, I promise," he continued. "Seven days of sun, fun and relaxation await us."

"Sounds great," she replied, forcing out a toothy smile. "Can't wait."

"It was French Polynesia, sir, was it not?" the pretty young woman behind the counter asked.

She flicked her dark curled hair to one side so that the ringlets cascaded down one shoulder and shot Jackson an overly flirtatious gaze from beneath poorly applied false lashes. She didn't even try to hide it. Elena wondered if she always made herself up like this, with the caking of fake tan and gaudy red lips. The red and cream cravat, that by the looks of the other staff was company uniform, did nothing to hide the ample cleavage that spilled out of her shirt from the button or two she had purposefully left undone, and almost onto the keyboard of her computer.

Slut must have known he was coming back, she mused. *Why do women act like this around him?*

And then something occurred to her as the girl tapped away on the keys. Who was the last person she remembered being like this with him? The girl in that café, maybe.

What was her fucking name?

And then it hit her.

Becky. She could see her smiling behind the counter. The name tag pinned to her chest. And her face plastered all over the news.

"That's correct," he replied, loving every ounce of the attention. "Tahiti or Bora Bora, we haven't decided yet. Elena, are you okay?"

Elena's face had gone as pale as a sheet. She closed her eyes and swallowed hard before answering.

"Perfect," she said, feigning interest. "Never better."

That was a lie. Inside, her mind was screaming at her to run. To get up and run as fast as she could away from him. She took a long, hard look at his face.

Is it really you? she thought. *After all this, has my dad been right all along? Are you the monster? How could I have been so stupid, so naïve?*

"Fantastic," Jackson said, putting a hand on one of her now trembling thighs. "So, which will it be?"

"What will which be?"

He leaned forward so that only she could hear him, drawing his eyes into narrow slits, and lowered his voice to a snarl.

"Please, don't embarrass me. I'm trying to do a nice thing. For us."

. . .

THE WIND, which had picked up significantly during their time indoors, whipped at the exposed skin on Elena's face and hands and chilled her right to the core. Her eyes watered, distorting her vision, and her lips began to tremble. Although, if she was honest, she hadn't much noticed. Her attention, what she had of it to spare at least, was focused solely on the man standing to her left. The man she felt as though she had terribly misjudged, and given far too much of herself to. The man who stood clutching holiday brochures, smiling, as though all was right in *his* world.

"Jackson, I..."

"You don't need to apologise."

"I wasn't... I mean I—"

He raised a palm to cut her off, shaking his head as if he were addressing a child he was displeased with.

"Perhaps you can redeem yourself ... tonight."

"Tonight?"

"I'm going to cook us dinner, back at my place, to celebrate booking this holiday. I'll pop and grab a bottle of wine for *you*. Why don't you get yourself something *nice* to wear, for *me*."

Jackson took her face in his hands and stroked down her cheek with the back of his fingers. She wanted to run, she wanted to vomit, but the power he held over her, fear, froze her to the spot.

"There's a good girl."

SHE SHOULD HAVE MADE her way to the train station, to a bus stop, to anywhere. She should have phoned her dad, or Ainsley, or Steve bloody Morgan for that matter. But she didn't. She needed to get to the bottom of whatever the hell was going on.

Elena browsed the rails and racks of the shop aimlessly, not really aware of what she was looking for, her eyes never fixing on a single item for long. The shop smelt of child sick and bleach. And, if she wasn't mistaken, someone had hidden a dirty nappy under a pile of jeans. A baby called out from behind her, and she nearly jumped out of her skin.

"Jesus fuck," she said aloud, holding her hand to her chest and earning an unappealing glare from its mother in the process. "Sorry," Elena said, giving the scowling a woman a smile.

Was she being watched, followed even? The feeling in her stomach said so, and the hairs on her neck and arms confirmed it. But there was no one there. Not to her left, right, or even behind her. She was still for a long moment, considering. She was gathering looks from passersby, but as far as she was concerned, they could all go and fuck themselves.

There will not be another victim, she told herself, standing tall now with her head high, newly invigorated, full of purpose, her green eyes burning with intent.

Elena looked to her left and picked up a half decent-looking cream floral dress from a sale rack. She eyed it up for size, and made her way to the cashier.

I NEED TO KNOW. I need to be sure.

40

"Maybe I *am* losing it. What if I'm looking at all the pieces in front of me, but they're all from the wrong puzzle?"

Ainsley took a long drink from her steaming mug before answering, using the time to study Graham's face from across the table.

"How do you mean?" she eventually asked.

"Maybe I just wanted it to be him ... Jackson. I wanted ... needed the case to be over quickly, to feel good about myself, and he fitted the bill."

Ainsley said nothing, but her expression was a prompt for him to explain further, which he grudgingly did after polishing off his coffee.

"Just because I think he's a bit of an oddball ..."

"Understatement of the century."

"Granted. But Elena's not stupid. She's *my* daughter, for Christ's sake. She wouldn't be seeing him if she thought he was some kind of nut job. Maybe after everything, I was just trying to protect *her*."

Ainsley moved to the sink, taking their empty cups with her, and flicked the kettle back on to boil. She stood, staring into the little garden beyond the window, and in a moment of silence, reflected. She enjoyed how Graham had landscaped the small space in his time off. And the small numbers of birds that had been attracted to the garden since its improvement. A pair of sparrows tussled with a blue tit over a pile of seeds and nuts on the new bird table that he had built, and the sounds they made soothed her.

"Or there could be another reason she's still with him," she eventually said, without turning from the window.

"I'm listening."

"What if... what if she *does* believe you."

Graham's ears pricked up as Ainsley spun around in a whirlwind of excitement to face him, nearly knocking the empty mugs to the ground.

"What if she's using her time to try to suss him out? Like you said, she is *your* daughter."

Graham reached for his phone, his eyes now full of worry and dread.

"Don't," Ainsley snapped. "If she is, then you cannot let on you know. Can't risk him knowing."

"Fuck. What have I got her into?"

THE DRESS, although a snap decision, hung from Elena's body with an effortless grace. It finished just above the knee and showcased the tattoos on her legs, and the subtle tones in its floral design paired perfectly with the textures in her hair and the green intensity of her eyes. She felt pretty. The shallowness of her breath gave away her nerves somewhat, but she did her best to hide them. However, this was the second time she had had to reapply her makeup already, the second time she had had to slip away into the bathroom to compose herself. Although the dress was thin and Jackson's flat airy, she was sweating pints.

You can do this, she told herself, as she stared at her own reflection in the back-lit mirror.

Jackson called from beyond the door for a third time. "Everything okay in there, beautiful?"

Even his voice now made her skin crawl. Being called "beautiful" was a punch to the gut. Elena pulled a sour grimace, holding back a gag by digging her nails into the palms of her hands.

"Yep, all good. I'll be out now," she managed.

Elena took a long, hard look at herself in the mirror, taking in every detail of her face, every line, every imperfection. She took a deep breath in, and a deep breath out, and turned for the door.

I've got this.

IN ELENA'S SHORT ABSENCE, Jackson had taken the opportunity to lay the table, pour wine, and light various candles around the imposing space. It was a shame, she thought, that the dinner was not under better circumstances, or in better company, because the setting itself was stunning.

The lighting had been turned down low and complemented the pretty sounds of Norah Jones that floated around the apartment. Beyond the full height windows, lights from the surrounding hotels and homes reflected off the still waters of the bay as the last of the evening's sun sank below the horizon. It really was quite beautiful here, something to behold.

"Elena?"

She turned to her left as her consciousness returned to the present. Standing, dressed in a tight-fitting light blue shirt, Jackson held out a chair for her at the table, with a glint in his eye that made her feel cold to the bone.

"Oh, I do love that dress on you."

"Thanks," she said with a feigned smile. "I don't half mind it myself."

Her phone lit up and vibrated loudly on the solid oak dining table. She could sense the displeased look on his face burning through her, so she turned it on silent and flipped the device over, looking back up to him with a smile as she did.

"I think..." he started slowly, taking a long draw from a glass of water before setting it down gently on the table, "I think it is time that you apologised, properly."

Fear gripped her. It thrust its hand into her chest and squeezed her heart and lungs. She was breathless as he motioned with his eyes and a single finger to the closed door of his bedroom.

"Jacks..." she replied shakily. "I thought the dress..."

He rose from his seat and motioned for her to lead the way. His face was cold, calculating, and there was no emotion in his eyes. He licked his lips before he spoke.

"Well then... shall we?"

As JACKSON'S bare form faded into the en-suite with a click of a door, Elena sat at the end of the bed, having only the torn remains of her dress to protect what was left of her fragile modesty. The feeling of violation bore no adjective, and she sat in silence as she heard him step into the shower. A single tear tracked down her cheek. Unconsciously, as the feeling of defeat overtook the waning adrenalin, she slipped from the end of the bed and onto the floor. But not with a thud. The sound was unfamiliar, hollow. She looked to her right, and to her surprise, found a dislodged floorboard.

Use your head, her dad said, in the back of her fuzzy and confused mind.

With a shaking and bruised hand, she lifted the board from its place. She strained her hearing towards the door. He was still in the shower. She reached a hand into the opening left in the floor, and pulled from it a small, aged wooden box.

Use your head, Graham continued.

She ran inquisitive fingers over the lid of the box. It bore markings, dinks, and dents. Whoever had made it had never taken the time to sand out any imperfections or workers' marks. A splinter caught in her finger, and she drew it back in pain. He was *still* in the shower.

Although not expecting to find fun-filled childhood memories, or a stuffed animal collection inside, when Elena did lift the lid on the box, she had to do her best not to vomit.

Phones. Dad's phone. Lewis' phone. With eyes wide, she dug further and further into what she now realised to be the box of horrors. Photographs of girls. Girls she recognised from the news. Taken from behind corners, from the inside of bushes and trees, photographs of their bodies, hand-written notes on them all. Sophie, Jessica, Becky, even photos of her, Elena, taken from outside of her bedroom window. Her hands shook, and she fought hard to fight back the waves of nausea or the compulsion to scream.

Jesus fuck, Dad was right.

Elena noticed the last girl in the photo from the travel agents. Jackson had marked it as *Caroline*, and she had been very much alive when she had seen her earlier that afternoon.

He's already chosen his next, she thought.

The sound of the shower being turned off was like a cold slap in the face, and she looked towards the door, heart racing, as she shoved the contents and the box back into its hole.

HE'S GOING to kill again.

41

THE BOY with the blue backpack took a seat on the end of his bed for one last time. He was taking a break, a breather, a moment to reflect on his time at the home before finishing packing his things. Jackson had been adopted, after all this time. And that afternoon, he would take his place alongside his new family.

It had been an odd few months for him. Odd, but weirdly beautiful. All told, apart from school, he had been pretty much left to his own devices. No one had bothered him. No one had tried to hurt him or call him names, to force him into a dark room or a waiting car. As a matter of fact, most people, particularly members of staff, had been giving him a rather wide berth. It appeared rumours had been spreading through the grim corridors and down the proverbial grapevine. The unexplained disappearances of a number of staff members, and an unusually high number of fatal accidents among their ranks recently, had only seemed to bolster and give credence to those claims. A fall here, a tumble there. Failed brakes on a car. Bleach in a coffee. It was strange then, that no police presence was ever seen at the home. Nor were those acts, sorry, those accidents, ever thoroughly investigated. As luck would have it, due to those misfortunes, or perhaps despite them, he had been pushed to the front of the queue, so to speak. As far as adoptions were concerned.

A young doctor and his pretty wife had taken a liking to him on their visit to the facility. They had praised his quick wit, charm, and manners, and had filled out the necessary paperwork before they had finished their tour that day. Eight weeks later, and they were coming to collect him. To take him home.

HE CLOSED the fasteners on the suitcase with an audible click, and ran a young hand up and across the peeling walls of his room. Old paint and plaster landed on the sheets of the bed as he ran his fingers in the grooves and cracks, across the words and memories carved into the deteriorating masonry.

I am finally free, he thought.

Tears gathered in his eyes as he glimpsed himself, distorted in the cracked mirror on the back of his door. He stood, and thrust a clenched fist into the middle of the mirror with a deafening scream. Shards of shattered glass landed at his feet and littered the carpet all around him. He imagined them to be memories. Memories that he had finally overcome. Memories that he had finally defeated. Jackson looked once more at the door where the mirror had once hung, the mirror where he had all too often seen his own bruised and bloodied face. And it was now empty. He put his palm to the bare wood of the door and laughed. A new start, a clean slate.

JACKSON ENTERED the reception area for the final time with his tattered blue backpack and suitcase in hand, and he found it to be empty. There was no one to see him off. No one to say goodbye and wish him well. And that was just fine. He could see the doctor standing beyond the heavy double doors, next to a car that would transport him far from this place, and onwards into his future.

He pushed the left-hand door with his free hand, and it opened reluctantly with a creak from its hinges. The winter cold bit at his face as the wind rushed by and ruffled his brown hair, the door slamming with a thud behind him as he let it go.

SEE YOU ALL IN HELL, he thought, as he walked towards the car.

42

SHE WEPT ALONE, and in silence. The unrelenting cascade of water from the shower drowned out all noise but itself. It spilled over her face and back, and through her hair that it had soaked through to her scalp. Elena sat with bare legs crossed, face covered by the drenched mats of her dreadlocks and admired the newly formed bruises that adorned her flesh. The insides of her thighs still throbbed and burned, and they, along with her wrists, were glowing many dark shades of purple.

Am I going to be just another victim, just another phone in a box? Just another annotated photograph?

The names and faces of those now confined to Jackson's little box plagued her mind, and she rocked back and forth, hysterically. The normally serene white of the shower tray now blackening with a mixture of mascara and blood. Her blood. *Their* blood.

Had she been blinded by the thought of love? Or at the

very least, lust? Had it blinded her to the point where she could not see who he really was, or what he was capable of? Had she been stupid enough to get sucked into his game, and stayed long enough for him to take it to his next level? She pondered on it, but her wounds were a testament to the fact.

What is he?

Elena wondered what the others had gone through, prior to being put on public display, before being exhibited to the world like freshly killed pigs at a weekly market. Had he played with them? Tortured them? Fucked *them* too? Had her contempt for her father, the one person who was trying to help her see sense, allowed Jackson to hunt close to her, and go about his ways almost unchecked?

Lewis' face, so young, so handsome and caring, flashed through her mind's eye. The thought of him was almost crippling, and she clutched at her throat, struggling to breathe, struggling not to vomit as she had done earlier. Would he come for her in the night, or would he wait? Would he play with her like a cat with a mouse until it was she who craved death? Until she herself embraced his twisted game with open and willing arms?

Elena lay in the shower, her bare and battered body shivering from the shock and the cold. She put her thumb to her mouth like a child and wept. She wept until she could no more, and then she slept.

"DAD," she whispered just as the sandman did his work, "Dad, I need you."

43

October 2nd 2018, 22:30

"Caroline is a beautiful name," Jackson said as he poured his date another glass of house white.

Her face blushed a shade of scarlet, but instead of shying away, she leaned in close to him. So close that he could smell her perfume, and almost taste her.

Now that I do like, he thought.

"Bit of luck then, really," she replied. "It's the only one I've got. I must say, I'm surprised you called so late."

"I had a space in my diary that I felt deserved filling."

Caroline raised her glass and drained it in one. She leaned back in her seat, just enough that her top rose just a little, to reveal her toned and tanned stomach to Jackson. He took the bait, and she heard him swallow.

"Does your girlfriend know where you are?"

He scoffed and smiled a wide, toothy smile. If arrogance had been visible, then it would have shot from his nose and landed in the shared breadbasket that sat between them both.

"She knows I'm a free man," he started, enunciating every word with care. "She knows I am free to do whatever, and *whoever* I damn well please."

The contents of his speech, however degrading, however vile, seemed very much to turn her on. She pursed her bright red lips as her body squirmed with excitement in the restaurant chair. Jackson thought that if they had not been in company, or for that matter a respectable eating establishment, that she would have already been over the table and mounting him.

We are keen, he thought, raising a finger in the air to gain the attention of a passing waiter.

"Can I help, sir?"

"Another bottle of the white for my lady friend please."

"Very good, sir, and for yourself?"

He looked at Caroline and smiled. "Oh, I have everything I need, thank you."

"FUCK, she's not answering her sodding phone."

"Graham, I thought you were going to leave it?"

He paced the living room, back and forth like a caged animal waiting for a meal. If he were there much longer, then Ainsley swore he would wear grooves the shape of his feet into the bare timber. "Something is wrong, Ainz, I can fucking well taste it. I can feel it in my very being that something is up."

He tapped the screen of his phone, once again dialling Elena's number. Still no answer.

"Stupid girl," he snapped.

Graham looked to the front door and made a beeline for his jacket hanging on the wall next to the key rack.

"Are you coming?"

"You're not going over there, Gray."

He threw the jacket on and shot a glance back at her; his eyes were wild and fierce, and they burned with a parental intensity. But she could see the distress behind them. The pain. The fear.

"No Ainsley, I'm not. *We* are."

44

————

THE SOUND of the Jeep's tyres screeching to a halt echoed down the noiseless street. It had never been the most subtle of cars; Graham had discovered that shortly after buying it. But now, here, in the soundless suburbs of Cardiff, he swore it could have woken the dead.

"Her bedroom light is on; she must be here," he said, slamming the car's door and throwing a half-finished cigarette to the ground.

He cupped his hands and called up to the window. "Elena!"

No movement. No reply.

Fuck.

Ainsley, still seated in the car, clutching on to her phone for dear life, was shocked to see Graham turn on his heels and stomp back in her direction, pointing a finger directly at her. She couldn't decipher what he was saying to her, through the steaming up glass and over the wind, so she had to open the door and lean out.

"What did you say, Gray?"

"Can you give me a hand? There's something in the boot I need you to help me with."

"In the boot?" She looked at him, completely bemused, and he just nodded.

Graham threw back a dust sheet that had been covering what he needed, and the pair both stood and stared.

"Where the bloody hell did you get it?" she asked, half confused, half impressed.

"Work. I would appreciate it if you didn't tell anyone, though. I have removed the serial numbers, but it's best if we just keep it between us."

"Uh... yeah, sure."

THE DOOR to Elena's apartment splintered into hundreds of pieces. Most of it landing in a pile in the hallway. The rest, what survived at least, came to rest against its hinges with a loud crack.

"Totally worth nicking it," Graham said as he laid the Sigma Enforcer battering ram on the concrete. "Remind me to throw it in a river after tonight, though. That wasn't exactly subtle."

"You got it," Ainsley replied with raised eyebrows and a half smile.

The pair rushed up the stairs to the main living area and found Elena, very much alive, something they were incredibly thankful for, curled up in a ball on her couch. She looked like hell. Soaking wet, naked, covered in purple bruises, one eye black from running make up, the other, from *him*.

"Jesus, Mary and fuck, Elena," Graham said as she came into view. He took off his jacket immediately to try and warm her.

"Ainz, can you go into her bedroom, get something warm, a blanket maybe?"

"I'm on it."

"Elena, kid, can you hear me?" he asked. "What the hell happened? Was it him? What has he done to you?"

She took her time, but eventually she came around, and managed her half-broken body into a seating position. As the sleep faded from her eyes, and she realised who it was that was beside her, with eyes wide, she burst into tears.

"Dad, I'm so sorry," she blurted out, throwing her arms around him. "You were right. You were right about everything."

THE THREE OF them sat around the small dining table that Elena normally used as a workstation. Ainsley had prepared them all coffee, and although she was now fully clothed, Elena was still shaking. Not only that, but she was essentially mute as well.

"Talk to me, kid. What the hell happened to you? And what did you mean by 'you were right?'" Graham said, setting a brightly coloured coffee mug on the table.

She said nothing, but stared deep into his eyes as her lips trembled. He could see behind hers, the green pools that made up her eyes, that she was hurting. She was hurting badly.

"Elena," he said, a little more forcefully this time.

"Graham don't," Ainsley said, cutting across him as she placed her hand on his.

Elena looked around her flat. She seemed to take in

every little detail as if she had never seen any of it before, as if it were alien to her. She exhaled deeply and took a long drink of the fragrant coffee.

"We can't talk, not here, not now."

"What? Why?" Graham asked.

She leaned in close and spoke in almost a whisper. "We don't know who else could be listening."

"Have you gone fucking mad?"

"Shh," she replied, thrusting a finger to his lips. "Not here. I'll get dressed and I'll meet you at your car. I heard that bloody thing coming a mile off."

Graham exchanged looks with Ainsley, whose eyes pleaded with him to trust his daughter. She squeezed his hand tighter, turned to Elena, and nodded.

"Fine. Five minutes," he eventually said after a long moment of consideration.

"Ten," Elena shot back. "No more, I promise."

"Ten," the others both agreed in unison.

Elena stood in front of the full-length mirror in her bedroom and let her father's jacket drop to the floor. She stood there and admired the reflection before her, and even let out a little grin. Elena looked after herself. The shape and composition of her form showed as much. But the marks and bruises he had left, the ones that were visible and the ones that were not, made her sick to her stomach. She blamed herself for everything, and she could have sworn that the reflection had pointed to each of the bruises and mouthed the words "you deserved this" at each one. She stood tall and held her head high, her eyes widening with intent.

"I'll make good on this," she said to her reflection. "On each and every one of these, that much I promise you."

"Where the sodding hell are you taking us?" Graham asked, spying the whites of Elena's eyes in the rear-view mirror.

"It's just around the next bend. There's a small gravel car park on the left."

The sound of the Jeep's chunky tyres floating across the gravel was the only sound, apart from the wind, to be heard for miles around. The trio got out of the car and braced themselves against the blowing gale. It was bitter, and would have nipped at any exposed skin that they might have had. Towering mountain peaks loomed in the inky darkness, but the sky was clear. And for miles around it was illuminated by countless stars and planets, and off on the horizon the city radiated its warming glow.

"What's this all about, Elena?" Graham asked, his voice barely audible over the wind. "Why are we here?"

"He shouldn't be able to hear us out here," she replied, looking off into the gloom.

"Who? Jackson?"

"Yes, fucking Jackson. Who else?"

"What's going on? What happened to you?" Ainsley asked, cutting across both them and the wind.

"You can both probably guess what happened to me. Neither of you are fools, and I won't waste your time, or mine for that matter, sharing any details." She looked down at the ground, almost ashamed, and lowered her voice. "That can wait for another time."

"Then why..."

"I'm getting there, Dad."

She took a deep breath to compose herself before delivering the news, the facts, the things that Graham had suspected but had until now been unable to prove. She paused because she knew the weight that her next words carried, the impact they would have. He wasn't going mad, or being paranoid. He probably had been drugged that night, and discounting all of his misgivings, he had been telling the truth about his drinking as of late, and she hadn't believed him.

"Dad, I am so, so sorry."

"Sorry about what, Elena?" His voice was becoming frantic now, pleading.

"YOU WERE RIGHT ABOUT HIM, about everything. And I can prove it."

45

"I'M SORRY?" Graham asked, not fully comprehending what Elena had said.

"All of it, Dad. I can prove it all."

If the wind had not been so deafening, then Graham and Ainsley's collective gasps would have filled the otherwise silent landscape. But in truth, the looks on their faces said it all.

"How?" Graham asked, his voice bordering on sounding harsh.

"He's kept trophies. From all of his victims. You included."

"Phones?"

"And photographs. Dad, he's sick, and he's planning another kill."

"Jesus Christ, who?" Ainsley asked across the roaring gale.

"A girl called Caroline. She works in the travel agent's in town. Dad, Becky worked in the café we all met in before. He was hunting then. He does it in fucking public, in plain view of the world."

Graham jabbed a finger at Elena. "I sodding well told you."

His voice sounded frantic, and the look behind his slowly filling eyes could have been taken for either anger or relief. Ainsley put herself between them and she forcefully pushed his arm down. He held her, and she him. He pulled her in tight and fully committed to their embrace before breaking down completely.

"I knew I wasn't losing it," he wailed. "Oh my god, Lewis—"

"Dad," Elena said, cutting him off mid-howl. "We can stop him, clear your name, and end this, all of it. I'm going to go back to him and get the evidence we need to end this prick."

"You mean you don't have it?" Ainsley said.

"No. But I will. No matter what it takes."

"Are you insane? Look what he's done to you already," Graham said as he wiped tears from his eyes.

"I refuse to be another victim. And if I can help it, there will be no others. But Dad..." She took a step forward and looked deep into his face, into his soul. "I need your help."

"Elena you're not—"

"Just shut up and let her speak, Graham," Ainsley snapped.

Taken aback by the harshness of Ainsley's tone and expression, he took a step back and fully evaluated the two pairs of eyes glaring at him. They pierced the blackness, the gloom of the landscape, and they made him feel exposed.

He was powerless against them, as though they stacked odds in their own favour, and plotted against him in the mist.

"We can get your job back. Get you out of that bloody squalor you call home. Get *you* back. We can put these ghosts to bed and let everyone's family finally grieve," Elena continued.

"That's all very well and good, but how?"

"I know where he keeps them, the trophies, and if I can get photographs of them, and send them to you, you can show Steve Morgan and come in on a white horse with the whole fucking cavalry."

Graham was silent for a long moment. He stood, facing out to the valley and the darkness below, considering. Considering his, and their, options, considering whether any of his past decisions had led them to *this*. Whether unknowingly, he had led Lewis to his death.

Graham turned and looked into the pools of his daughter's eyes. The wind whipped around her, blowing her hair in all directions, making her appear frenzied and out of control. But he saw in her eyes there was nothing but peace and calm. She had an air of power and authority about her at that moment. She was *in* control. But he would not put her in danger's way, not if he could help it.

"There might be another way…"

"Dad, no…"

"Let me sleep on it, Elena. Let me think. You don't need to be the hero if it can be helped."

"I'm not trying to be a bloody hero…"

"Good," he cut right across her. "Then let me think about it. You can stay with me tonight; I don't want you in the flat by yourself."

Elena pouted like a child who had been sent to bed early, and without dinner. She crossed her arms and puffed out her lips in disgust.

"Less of that, please. Now come on, let's go, it's bloody arctic up here and I'm freezing my nuts off." He motioned with his hands for them both to follow him back to the waiting car.

"Dad..."

"Graham, perhaps..." Ainsley started.

"Not now, please. Just get in the fucking car, Elena."

THE TOAST JUMPED from the toaster with an audible 'pop' and filled the kitchen with wonderful smells. Graham had not long eaten, but the aroma made his stomach rumble, and mouth water.

Graham sat the breakfast down on the table in front of Elena, and he himself took a seat with a coffee. He drank deeply, enjoying the buzz of the caffeine, before turning to her to speak.

"I've not long got off the phone with Steve... with DCI Morgan. I'm meeting with him early this afternoon. I don't know if we have enough for a warrant. But we can try."

"That's great..."

"But... I need you to promise me you'll stay away from him. From all of this."

She nodded her head as she drank from her cup, defeated.

"I need to hear you say it, Elena."

"I got it," she said, sincerely. "I promise."

"Thank you."

Graham rose from the table and continued to butter a

second round of toast. Elena was a messy eater, and the stray crumbs from her mouth had made it from the table to the floor, and subsequently between the toes of his bare feet. He chuckled to himself.

I'll let it go this once, he thought. *Just this once.*

46

October 3rd 2018, 16:45

Jackson took the door by its handle, swinging it open lazily on the full arc of its hinges. He stood there, silent, radiating a smile that seemed to scream victory. He scoffed, releasing his grip from the handle and placing that hand in the pocket of his jeans as the door came fully to rest against the wall.

"Can I come in?"

He stood to one side, in such a way to allow just enough space for Elena to pass between his body and the door frame. He was standing far too close to her for her liking. So close that he towered over her, as if he were *trying* to appear intimidating.

As if he needed to try, she thought.

His apartment smelt different. There were all the usual aromas: lavender cleaner and incense, fine leather, and oak furniture. And due to the lack of current personal space at present, Jackson's hot breath. But there was something else.

Something new. It was women's perfume. A cheap, nasty floral scent. And it wasn't hers.

You've already had her here, haven't you? Jesus, is she still alive?

Elena's eyes darted to all corners of the room, searching for something, anything that confirmed her suspicions, or better yet, deny them. Jackson moved his body to meet her eyes. His stare was icy cold, wide, and unblinking. Did he suspect *her*? Already?

"You know how I feel about you, Jacks," she eventually said, trying her best to stem any shakiness in her voice and appear sincere.

"Let's just clear one thing up first." Jackson's voice was as cold as his stare, almost robotic. "You left without saying goodbye the other day."

"I had to go..."

He lifted his hand with his index and middle fingers raised and shushed her. "It was incredibly rude. And if *this* is going to continue, it will never happen again. Am I clear?"

Are you shitting me? she thought.

"I... I guess," she replied, not covering her fear quite as well that time.

"I need you to promise." He enunciated every word, slowly flaring his nostrils as he spoke.

"I... I promise."

"Wonderful."

Jackson gave her a wide smile, and his voice softened. He took Elena by the arm, kissing her on the forehead as he did, and began to lead her towards the kitchen. Lucky for her she had chosen to wear her baggy dungarees that sat away from her skin, because she was sweating like hell, and it was taking all of her power to keep her breathing under control, and her hands from shaking.

What am I doing? she thought.

"You are in luck, young lady." The charming, handsome young man from weeks past was back in the room, and it was disturbing how quickly he could change.

"I have not long got back from the supermarket. I've picked up some ingredients. I thought we would cook dinner together. Sound fun?"

She offered him what smile she could, and she hoped to hell that it was enough. Because inside she was having regrets. Regrets about being there. Regrets about being with him. Regrets about not listening to her father.

I suppose this is what I get for trying to help.

"S...sounds great, Jacks. What are we having?"

THE SIGHT of him handling a blade, especially one that large, turned her blood cold. But even she had to admit that watching him prepare vegetables *was* impressive, but not surprising given the extent and scale of his *other* work. The aroma of sautéed onions and garlic filled the kitchen. For a moment, Elena forgot why she was there. Things between them had been good at one point. Really good. And the fact that she'd let his darker side pass her by for so long began to kind of make sense. He could be normal. Or at least act that way, very convincingly. He was hiding in plain sight, and my god was he good at it.

"Smells great, Jacks."

"It's getting there. Pass me that balsamic and we'll really get this bird singing."

Each time he passed her, he made a conscious effort to squeeze a body part or kiss her softly. Even now, under those circumstances, he still had the power to make her go weak at the knees. As much as it astonished her, as it had the first time they had met, now it made her feel ashamed.

Head and heart. Think with your head and heart. Remember why you are here. Remember their faces.

"I'll set the table, shall I?"

Anything to take a breath, she thought.

He stopped mid-stir and took her chin in his hand as she passed. He examined the bruises on her face. He looked smug, as if he was almost proud of what he had done to her.

"I'll try to be gentler next time."

Next time?

Elena placed knives next to forks, napkins next to glasses, and plates next to bowls. All the while wishing he would leave, just for a moment, to use the bathroom, get something from the car. Hell, go and fuck Caroline if it meant she could get into the bedroom. She only needed a few seconds in there, and she could end him.

The hairs on the back of her neck stood on end. He was watching her from the kitchen. She could feel it. Elena could no longer hear the sound of utensils on saucepans, but she could hear his footsteps. They were careful, deliberate, and they were getting louder, getting closer. She didn't turn to meet his gaze, but she knew he was standing right behind her. She could almost taste his breath.

"Look at me," he said, again with that cold, calculated tone.

Elena did so, slowly. Her heart was pounding in her chest. Was this it?

"You truly are beautiful, Elena."

"Th... thanks."

"I have decided that dinner can wait."

"You have? Wait for what?"

"For me to be satisfied."

Elena's breath left her body.

"The bedroom," he said. "Five minutes. Be naked."

Jackson muttered his final command and made his way across the apartment, through the door to the bedroom and into the en-suite. He closed the door behind him, and Elena heard the shower turn on.

She knew what had to be done, and this was as perfect an opportunity as she was likely to get. But fear had frozen her to the spot. Her legs would not move.

Move. Fucking move.

One foot in front of the other. One ear to the bathroom. Sweat beads dripped the length of her face, dropping to the floor like rain drops. One foot in front of the other. One ear still to the bathroom. Her heart was pounding so heavily that she struggled to listen. She could still barely hear the shower, cascading from its head. He was still in there, still moving around. A few more steps.

Elena reached the bed and knelt on the floor.

Let's end this, she told herself, as she removed the floorboard, and subsequently the small wooden box.

She reached a hand into the pocket of her dungarees and retrieved her phone, snapping photos of each trophy as fast as she could.

New message –

Dad new phone.

Send photos.

The apartment was now silent. The shower cascading no more. And Elena felt the same cold feeling creep the length of her spine as the hairs on her neck stood on end.

"Well, isn't this interesting?" Jackson's voice came from behind her. He sounded excited, playful almost.

He was on her in an instant, before she could react. He grabbed a handful of her golden dreadlocks and thrust her backwards, headfirst into the wall. Elena slumped onto her side, motionless.

Jackson knelt beside her unmoving form and moved his neck to one side with an audible click. He picked up the phone, cradling it between his still-damp fingers, and smiled.

Incoming Call – Dad.

"Elena. Hello. Are you there?"

"I THINK we should play a game. Don't you agree, Detective Walker?"

47

THE LINE WAS quiet for a long moment. Quiet, all except for the heavy breathing of the two men at either end of the phone.

"I said, what the hell have you done with her, freak?" Graham was almost screaming, and his voice was breaking. "If you lay even a single finger on her..."

"Oh, I can assure you that I have already done much more than *that*. Do you wish for me to describe how she tastes? Or perhaps how well she fucks. You know, she actually enjoys being slapped around a bit. It gets her all riled up and mad-eyed."

"One more word from you, I swear."

"Oh, come now, Graham, save your breath. It's going to be a long night otherwise. If I were you, I would save your strength. You're going to need it, old man. Now, if you don't mind, I must dash. I have a guest to attend to and preparations to make. Ta-ta."

With a click, the line went dead.

Graham leapt across the living room and snatched his jacket, holding the phone to his ear as he did.

"Gray, talk to me. What's going on?" Ainsley said as he rushed past her.

"Dammit, Steve, answer your sodding phone."

"Graham, please," she continued, pleading.

"Useless prick," Graham barked at his phone.

He looked up from the illuminated screen and was met by Ainsley's terrified face. In the panic, he had all but forgotten she was there, for he was consumed by fear and guilt.

"He's got her. Jackson has Elena."

No words left her trembling mouth. The only movement on her face was a single tear that tracked down her left cheek, leaving behind eyes that sparkled and shook in terror and disbelief.

"But she... she's upstairs, isn't she?"

Graham stole a glance at his watch.

"If we leave now, we should be able to catch Morgan in the office. That psycho has my daughter. And we are going to need as much help as we can to get her back."

"She could be anywhere. He might have already..."

"Elena is alive. For now, at least. I'll bet on it. He thinks this is a game."

"How can you be certain?"

"I just know. Arseholes like him enjoy this. He'll make an example of her."

Graham took Ainsley lightly by the hand and offered her what weary smile he could. He pulled her in close and kissed her.

"Come on, we'd better get a move on."

. . .

ELENA LAY THERE, in her own personal dark, and wondered what the others felt when they were here. Where they even offered such a courtesy? Her hands and feet were bound, she was gagged and blindfolded, but she knew where she was. The motion gave it away, but if not that, then it would have been the stench. He had cleaned it thoroughly, no doubt about it, but there was no masking death. It was not just a smell, it left behind memories, it left behind fears. And in the boot of Jackson's car, blindfolded as she was, she could almost taste it.

The thumping in her head was made worse by the road noise. More than once since she had regained consciousness the sound had changed, as had the feeling of the vibrations that ran through her body from the tyres.

Where are we?

It was no use trying to string together the lefts and rights. There was no way of telling how long they had been driving while she was out.

The road had been pothole-ridden and bumpy at first. Start, stop. Start, stop. And now it was continuous, but the hum was louder.

The motorway maybe? Heading out of the city?

Her mouth was *so* dry, and the bonds were hurting her wrists and ankles. They had chafed some miles back, but now that mild discomfort had become outright agony. It wouldn't be long, she thought, until her hands and feet were as sticky from blood as the wound on her head.

I wonder what he'll do with me. The same as Jessica? As Becky? Or worse?

Elena lay motionless and contemplated the roller-coaster of emotions that her father must now be experiencing. A fear so pronounced that it bore no name. A feeling of helplessness that would be debilitating, almost crippling, game-ending for most. How would she react if the roles had been reversed? She hoped that what she had managed to get to him would be enough. Enough at least to clear his name, if nothing else. She was done for, that was a given, but perhaps her suffering, and the torment that was about to follow, would not be in vain.

"Ergh, Walker, what the hell are you doing here?"

DCI Morgan was in the middle of briefing the team on the current progress of various cases, his chubby finger pointing at the whiteboard, when Graham and Ainsley burst into the Bull Pen.

"Steve," Graham called out as he breached the threshold, panting for breath. "He's got her. He's got Elena."

THE DOOR of Morgan's office slammed behind them as they entered. His face did nothing to hide how he felt in Graham's presence, and he opened his mouth to give some comfort, to try to console the man who had once been his friend. That was, until Ainsley thrust a phone screen in his face.

"What the fuck is this? What am I looking at?"

"Evidence, Steve. Evidence that shows I was right."

"Right about what?"

"Jackson bloody Page."

The colour drained from Morgan's face and he took an instinctive step back, gasping as his body contacted the desk. The inertia knocked his picture frame from its spot and onto the floor, shattering the glass.

"How... how many?" His voice was shaky now, and all

the anger was completely gone, replaced now with shock. Shock, guilt, and perhaps even horror.

"All of them. The four we know of. More perhaps," Ainsley said.

"He has Elena. Steve," Graham repeated, taking a step closer to him. "He is going to kill my little girl."

48

"All units, this is Detective Chief Inspector Steven Morgan," he said over the radio.

The car tore through the bustling streets of Cardiff, weaving in and out of traffic, parked cars, and pedestrians. Its single blue flashing light illuminated what little corners of the metropolis that were not bathed in streetlight. The engine roared as Graham shifted through the gears, but to him it was silent. Not even the wail of the siren, or the barked commands of Morgan, pierced his consciousness. He was fixated on one thing. You could have called it tunnel vision; and when the drive was over, when they arrived at their destination, would he have remembered any of it at all?

Morgan continued, "Suspect is an IC1 male, early thirties, with long brown hair. Thought to be in possession of one Elena Robinson. Suspect is considered dangerous, so do not approach without the appropriate backup. Last known location was the suspect's residence. Do not enter the premises until all units are on site."

He dropped the radio receiver back into its holder and turned to Graham, who had not said a word since the three of them, Ainsley included, had taken the unmarked car, and sped out of the station a few minutes before.

"Techies are trying to get a fix on Elena's phone. Fingers crossed, she still has it on her, or at the very least he has it. If we come up blank at Page's address, then at least we won't be standing around with our fingers up our arses. We'll get her back, Gray. That much I promise you."

Some distance away, the glare and bustle of civilisation had succumbed to winding, empty roads and silence. Darkness was around every bend, every corner, and the car's head-lights only barely pierced the gloom. Soft music played on the radio, and the driver, relaxed and smiling as he was, hummed along to the pleasant tune.

He was in no rush.

Better to be tardy than dead, he thought with a morbid grin.

The occasional 'thump' from the rear of the vehicle did nothing to dampen his spirits. He followed each one with a quick glare in the rear-view to check all was fine, and the words "Oh you," he said with an adoring chuckle. Jackson was having a wonderful evening, and it had only just begun.

"Oh, how I wish we could have made this work," he said, looking into the rear-view mirror, addressing his passenger in the back. "For a while I thought you saw me, like actually saw me for who I was, who I truly am beneath this false exterior. But I was mistaken. Such a pity that is for us both."

As the car climbed higher into the hills and above the

lingering cloud, the peaks of the Brecon Beacons loomed into view. Contrasted against a starlit sky, the monoliths of rock and ice dominated the horizon. It was here, nestled between the summits, that a familiar place, for Jackson at least, lay. It had been defiled by outsiders recently, the unworthy, and they had poked and prodded around. They had come to judge, to try and paint a picture of him, to understand him with their limited view. Although he had led them there, as a test, to see how well they would do, which was poorly, he had for a time wondered whether it was all a mistake.

"We won't have much time alone together, I'm afraid. They know this place, and although I mock them, they are not totally inept, not all of them at least."

Jackson turned to his left and placed a hand on the small wooden box that lay on the passenger's seat, and he stroked it tenderly.

Not your father, I fear, he thought.

THE ENTRANCE DOOR to Jackson's apartment exploded into a shower of wooden splinters as it was knocked clean from its hinges by the battering ram.

"Police, police, police." The sound echoed around the enormous open plan space as the officers entered. The view that greeted them was as far away from the refuge of a twisted killer as they could have expected. A luxury executive flat that extended out of view in every direction, with views of the bay that were the stuff of an advertiser's dream.

"Page!" Graham called out, frantically flying from one corner of the home to the other. "Elena!"

He came to stop in the entrance way to the bedroom and gazed down at the empty hole in the floor. The hole that would have once housed the trophies, the keepsakes of a man who appeared on the surface to be so normal. The memorabilia of a psychopath who had become as adept at blending in, as proficient in wearing a suit of normality as he was at taking life. He took a second to look around, and noticed, as vomit entered his mouth and fear clutched at his throat, a cracked section of plasterboard dotted with crimson. A small bunch of blonde hair sat in a neat bundle on the floor beneath.

His heart sunk and he fought to hold back the tears. *Elena. Where are you?*

"There's no one here, sir," one of the uniforms announced after completing their sweep of the property, addressing both Graham and DCI Morgan simultaneously. "But... but there is something you'll both want to see."

Nestled between the pillows of Jackson's bed was a mask. The mask of a lamb. And on it, written in blood, was a single word.

Elena.

The blood in Graham's veins turned to ice. And he shot a look to Morgan, whose own face mirrored Graham's fears. He took a step forward, and upon taking the mask in hand, a single tear tracked the length of his exhausted and weather-beaten face.

"Sir."

A young, uniformed officer clambered into the home, visibly out of breath from running up the many flights of stairs. She fought for breath as she struggled to speak.

"Sir...they're ..."

"Spit it out, constable," Morgan barked.

"Give her a second, Steve." Graham took a step towards the officer, mask still in hand, and offered her a weary smile.

"Sir, it's Page. We've got a fix on Miss Robinson's phone. Sir, they're up in the Beacons."

"Back to the cars," Morgan ordered.

"Sir, that's not all," the constable continued. "There's something else you should know."

THE SOUND of rubber running over gravel broke the lingering silence in the valley. Jackson opened the driver's door and took in a lungful of the crisp mountain air. He smiled, and his smile was met by the 'hoot' of a far-off tawny owl.

Home, he thought as he stood in awe of the location, and stretched the journey out from within his joints and muscles. *It is nice to be home.*

He swung around to the back of the car and opened the boot. Gazing down, he saw a pair of green eyes staring back at him, thrusting would-be daggers through the cavity in his chest.

"I see you removed the blindfold. Bravo."

Jackson raised his right hand, in which he held the small wooden box. He thrust it forward just enough so that Elena could see it. He shook it and smiled.

"COME ON, we have some people we would like you to meet."

49

———

"SOME OF THE guys back at the station started doing some extra digging around when the call came in," the female officer continued, wedged in the back of the car between a window and Andrews. "You know, double, triple checking things. And they noticed something."

"As much as I am enjoying the sound of your voice, constable, do us all a favour and get to the point," Graham said, squeezing the car between the posts of a cattle grid at speed.

"Sir," she nodded. "I don't know how we could have missed it. It's Page. He was adopted when he was a teenager. His birth parents died in a murder-suicide when he was a child. 'Page' wasn't his birth name."

Morgan turned on his spot, twisting his head over the back of the headrest. "What are you saying?"

"His name is – *was*, Jackson Thomas."

"Thomas," Graham said. "Why does that ring a bell?"

Ainsley pushed herself forward, free of the pincer-like grip of Andrew's stomach and the window. "It's because 'Thomas' was the name of the family who used to own the cottage that we are now driving towards."

"Jesus," Graham said, swerving to miss a clearly nocturnal sheep. "So, it's *his* bloody house."

"I HAVEN'T REALLY CHANGED a thing here since I was old enough to come back," Jackson said as he paced across the slate tiled floor. "They liked it like this, and they worked hard for it, so who would I be to change it, to alter what they saw as perfection?"

He dragged a finger across the rotting worktops of the kitchen as he spoke, stopping only to steal a gaze skywards through the hole in the roof, and into the star-studded heavens that hung silently overhead.

Elena stared at him, with a mixture of concern, confusion, and cold, distilled fear. He had left the blindfold off, not that that comforted her, as her bound hands were now held above her, hooked across a piece of corroded metal that had been hammered into the stone wall. She could barely feel them now. If she were honest, the blood had drained from them, and her arms were now all but numb. Even her heart had stopped racing, and her breathing was now almost what could be considered normal. It was as though her body had already succumbed to the inevitable, and her conscious mind was now nothing more than a passenger, a viewer along for the ride.

Just get on with it, she thought.

She screamed at him. She spat the last of her venom with what little fight she had left in her. But through the rag in her mouth, nothing more than muffled cries could be deciphered. Her eyes burned at him, and for the first time in her life, she actually wished another person dead.

"How far away are we?" Graham asked.

Consulting the maps on her phone, she again pushed forward. "Twelve minutes," Ainsley said.

"Put the fucking siren back on. Let this prick *know* we're coming," Morgan added.

"No, Jesus Christ – don't. We don't know how fragile he is. You don't want to push him into action, to force his hand," Ainsley said.

Flicking his dead cigarette out of the window, Graham immediately reached for another and lit it. He was silent for a brief moment before answering, before even physically showing any reaction to the conversation happening around him. He just pushed forward, his mind and his gaze fixed on nothing but the road that stretched out before him. Nothing but the road, and what lay at the end. *Elena.*

"We stay quiet," he eventually said, not addressing anybody in particular. "He knows we are coming, otherwise he would have ditched Elena's phone. The only thing we have is that he doesn't know exactly when."

"Shh, shh," Jackson said softly, putting his index finger to Elena's lips. "They like it quiet here. That's why we moved out of the city, to get away from it all."

He knelt down in front of her so that his eyes met hers. He reached for the gag and took it gently between his fingers.

"Are you going to be quiet?" he asked, looking deep into her eyes. He was so close now she could almost taste him.

"I'll take your silence for compliance. Let's keep it that way, shall we?"

He stood up, his gaze still fixed on her face, and tossed the damp rag to the floor.

"Water," Elena choked out. "Please, Jacks, I need water."

Ignoring her request, Jackson made his way back towards the kitchen units. He placed a hand on the wooden box, appearing to fill full of light as he did, and looked skyward.

"Jacks?" Elena pleaded.

"Shall we introduce her?" Jackson asked, aiming the question at the box. "You think so?"

"Jackson, what are you on about? Look at me, please."

"Quiet," he snapped, his eyes momentarily filling with anger. "You should be grateful for this. Shouldn't she, Mother?"

Mother?

Jackson stood in the middle of the kitchen, eyes closed, with a wide, toothy smile on his face. He held his hands to his chest, as if he were cradling his own heart, his smile growing with each passing second.

"You're right, she is a beauty. She is very special indeed." He spoke without opening his eyes. "What's that? Oh yes, highly intelligent too. A real all-round catch."

"Jackson." Elena's pleas broke into sobs, but he wasn't listening.

"She'll fit well with the others, I'm sure. We have all spoken about it at great length."

His face changed, and his voice became defensive.

"Well, of course I was going to consult you first, that's why she's here. No ... Mother, listen."

"You're fucking sick," Elena screamed, forcing out the words with all of her might.

His eyes opened. He stared, glared right through her for a second, and then he reacted. In a single concise movement, Jackson turned on the spot, took a plate from the counter, and hurled it in Elena's direction. It contacted the stone wall inches above her head. Elena let out a scream of terror as shards of porcelain rained down around her.

"Keep quiet," he spat, as he rewound his body into its original position. "Can you not see that I'm having a conversation?"

THE UNMARKED CAR sat idle at the crossroads. Its engine a comforting hum against the backdrop of silence. Clouds were gathering overhead, and the visibility, although never great, diminished by the second.

"Left or right? Anybody?" Graham asked, frantically tapping his fingers against the steering wheel. "I need an answer, guys."

Everyone else in the car was busy, some tapping away at phones, others trying to read years-old maps in less-than-ideal lighting.

"There's no signal out here, Gray. I can't access the maps," Ainsley choked out, tears gathering in her eyes.

Graham took a deep, long breath. He filled his lungs with the crisp mountain air from the open window, and he closed his eyes. He blocked out all sound and concentrated only on his breath.

Left or right, Elena? Left or right?

Breathe in, breathe out.

Left, or right?

Breathe in, breathe out.

Memories of Elena as a baby, as a child and then a young woman came flooding into his mind. Happy memories, funny memories, memories that caused him pain. All came into his mind in a tidal wave of emotion. A tidal wave that focused his mind. He gripped the steering wheel tighter.

Breathe in, breathe out.

His eyes snapped open.

Left.

"FUCK YOU," she screamed, spitting the words like venom. "You're nothing but a sick, pathetic murderer."

"Oh, did you hear that mother? She thinks she has me all figured out." He turned his gaze to Elena. "Well, let me tell you, you're wrong."

"If you're going to kill me, just get it over with. I've seen enough of your face for one lifetime already."

Jackson erupted into a fit of laughter. "Oh, isn't she just a darling? So entertaining. No. No, you are going to suffer. By the time I'm finished with you, death will not be enough to quench your pain. And on that note, if you will just sit tight, I need some supplies from the car."

"Jackson," she screamed as he left.

Think Elena, think.

She scanned the room for something, anything, to help her escape. Nothing. Rain fell from the sky, through the hole in the roof.

Dad, if you are ever going to be a hero, now would be the time.

Elena gazed skywards as a droplet of water landed on her head. And she noticed something. Her bindings were fraying on the sharp edges of the corroded metal. She rubbed frantically.

Come on, you fucking things, come on.

Faster and faster, she rubbed. Sweat poured from her brow and her heart was racing. She kept one ear to the door.

Come on.

He was coming.

"I'm so glad you stuck around," he said as he came back through the door, placing an old blue rucksack down as he passed the kitchen worktops. "I wouldn't want you to miss this."

Think Elena.

Think.

"I bet your parents have never missed you."

Caught off guard, Jackson turned to face her.

"I'm sorry, what did you say?"

"You heard me. I bet they left you alone on purpose. They must have seen you like I do. Pathetic. I bet your mother wished she would have swallowed."

Rage. It filled him from his feet to his forehead. He began to shake, and one of his eyes twitched.

"Take it back."

"They look down on you and laugh. Your dad should have spilled you on your whore mother's tits."

Jackson flew across the room, his feet barely contacting the slate floor. He picked Elena up by the arm pits and slammed her into the tile.

"Bitch. Lying bitch," he screamed.

The motion of hitting the floor snapped the final strands of Elena's bindings.

"Stupid, lying cow." He was so close to her that saliva splashed on her face as he spoke. "I'm going to enjoy watching you bleed."

Elena patted around for something to defend herself with, finding a shard of broken porcelain next to her leg.

"Mother, are you watching?"

As he lifted his head to speak, Elena thrust the shard of plate into him, and it found home in the soft flesh of his shoulder.

He recoiled in horror, clawing at his wound, as blood seeped through his shirt and onto his hands. He hit the kitchen cupboard and slumped back, and laughed hysterically.

Elena darted for the door. But he was on her. He tackled her to the floor, taking her down by her legs. Her head kissed the slate tile with a sickening thud.

"You're making this more fun than even *I* deserve, Elena."

Her vision was blurry, and she could only just make out the outline of his form in the dark. But she could hear him. She could hear the poison seeping from between his lips.

From outside, there was the faint sound of rubber on gravel.

"Finish it," she said in a whisper. "Go on, finish it."

Jackson scoffed. "What's the hurry?"

He pulled the shard of dinner plate from his shoulder with a wince. Holding it, inspecting it under the moonlight, he watched as the crimson liquid sparkled and dripped on his hand. His breathing shallowed.

He stood above her, panting for breath, his blood-stained hands shaking from the adrenalin.

"No," he replied quietly. "You do not deserve a quick or peaceful death."

He laughed harder now, pointing one finger at her as his other hand clutched at his wound.

"Just like your father. Never able to get things finished. I was right about that at least. You're just like him."

"You know nothing about me."

"You and him, what a pair of pitiful cunts."

The rubber on gravel became footsteps as he brandished the shard, thrusting it ever closer to her.

"You are going to suffer."

The front door swung open with a crash.

"Elena!" a voice cried out.

"Police, police, police," echoed several more.

Panicked, Jackson threw the shard to the floor and rapidly made for the back door, sparing only a fleeting glance back to his prize on the tile.

"I'll be back for you, Elena."

He spun as the encroaching footsteps got louder, and snatched the back door open. He took a step outside, and the brisk evening air kissed at the bare skin of his face, and he savoured a lungful. But as he took another agitated step forward and away from her, a figure emerged from the shadows.

"Going somewhere, Page?"

Jackson stopped dead. And as he did, a pair of glimmering blue eyes glared back at him from the gloom.

And he chuckled.

"GOOD EVENING, DETECTIVE WALKER."

50

"YOUR MAN, Walker, will he be on side? Will he be a team player?"

The slender man in a fine-cut suit leaned back into his chair, placing his crystal wine glass down on an antique oak desk.

"He'll play ball."

"He had better do, Steven. I am putting a lot of faith in you. *We* are putting a lot of faith in you. You don't want to disappoint us again now, do you?"

Morgan shifted uncomfortably in his chair, wishing now that he had accepted the offer of a stiff drink.

"He won't be a problem."

"Well, you should hope not. His predecessor asked a few too many questions. That didn't sit well with us, and look what happened to him. Very sad, and with two young children."

The man stood from his desk and turned his back on

Morgan. He stared from beyond a large window, wine glass in hand, to the pounding waves and rocks below.

"These cliffs can be treacherous, Steven. Remember that. Best you keep yourself on this side of the precipice."

Morgan rose from his chair and wiped the sweat from his palms down the fronts of his trousers. He was red in the face, and it did nothing to hide his anxiety. The man turned to face him, a wide, wild smile adorning his face.

"Does he know?" the man asked.

"He will, if the time calls for it."

"WONDERFUL. Well, it seems we're all winners then." He raised his glass to Morgan and laughed. "To new friends."

EPILOGUE

THE EARLY SPRING sun kissed Elena's face. The breeze was significant, but pleasant. It came off the ocean and brought with it a gentle spray. The comforting sounds of holidaying families was mixed with the frantic calling of seagulls. That, in itself, was calming.

They sat snuggled into one another on a bench at the end of the pier. They looked out to the ocean and to the horizon beyond, reflecting on times past, and those events which had yet to happen. The sun shone brightly, but winter had left behind a chill in the air, a reminder of months gone by.

"You okay there, kid?" Graham asked, pushing his hands into his pocket.

"I am. Yeah, I'm okay, thank you."

Graham's phone vibrated, and he stole a quick glance at its screen.

"Is that work?" Elena asked, looking at him from beneath a chunky beanie, her green eyes sparkling.

"Page has admitted to everything. According to this," he

said, referring back to his screen, "he's being transferred to Ashworth until his sentencing. You're safe, kid. I promise. It's over."

She said nothing, but smiled and cast her gaze back to the ocean. Elena was silent for a long moment.

"He'll never get what he deserves," she said eventually. "There is not a thing that could make what he has done right. People will love him, revere him even, for what he did. I bet he's already receiving fan mail. People seem to love a good murderer."

"People are sick. They're fascinated by the twisted minds of killers. Nothing new there. You wait, there'll be a bloody film about him in time."

Elena laughed. "And who will play you?"

"Johnny Depp. No question."

"You're a bit fat, aren't you?"

"Cheeky cow," he chuckled. "They'll probably get a body double."

"Body triple more like."

The pair burst into fits of laughter, with Graham playfully trying to remove Elena from her seat. She responded by punching him on the arm.

"What am I missing here?"

Ainsley took a seat next to Graham, passing a cup of steaming coffee to each of them in turn.

"Just this poor old man being abused by the younger generation, nothing new."

ELENA TOOK a long drink from the polystyrene cup, looked at the people by her side, and once more to ocean at her front.

"This move will be good for us. Good for us all."

Graham sat back and put an arm each around Ainsley and Elena.

"I don't doubt it, kid. I don't doubt it for a second. We could all do with a fresh start."

READERS CLUB

Join my readers club to receive a free Book: *Fledgling - DI Graham Walker Prequel Novella.*

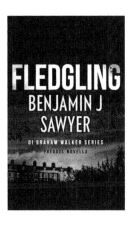

It's completely free to sign up and you will never be spammed by me, you can opt out easily at any time.

To join, head over to - www.benjaminjsawyer.com

PLEASE LEAVE A REVIEW!

If you have enjoyed this book, it would be great if you were able to leave a review.

Reviews help me gain visibility and they can bring my books to the attention of other readers who may enjoy them.

Thank you in advance, Ben.

Printed in Great Britain
by Amazon